**monsoon**books

## SPIRIT TIGER

Barbara Ismail spent several years in Kelantan in the 1970s and '80s, living in Kampong Dusun and Pengkalan Cepa, studying Wayang Siam and the Kelantanese dialect. She holds a PhD in Anthropology from Yale University, and is originally from Brooklyn, New York.

*Spirit Tiger* is the third in Barbara Ismail's series of Kain Songket Mysteries based in Kelantan. The first book in the series, *Shadow Play*, won Best Debut Novel at the 2012 SBPA Book Awards in Singapore and was shortlisted for the Popular–The Star Readers' Choice Awards 2013 in Malaysia; the second book in the series, *Princess Play*, was shortlisted for the Popular–The Star Readers' Choice Awards 2014 in Malaysia.

For more information about the author and her books, visit *www.barbaraismail.com*.

Kain Songket Mysteries
(published and forthcoming)

*Shadow Play*
*Princess Play*
*Spirit Tiger*
*Moon Kite*
*Western Chanting*
*Little Axe*

# SPIRIT TIGER

Volume III in the Kain Songket Mysteries Series

BARBARA ISMAIL

monsoon

**monsoon**books

Published in 2015
by Monsoon Books Pte Ltd
www.monsoonbooks.com.sg

Editorial / Sales:
No.1 Duke of Windsor Suite, Burrough Court,
Burrough on the Hill, Leics. LE14 2QS, UK

Registered office:
150 Orchard Road #07-02, Singapore 238841

First edition.

ISBN (paperback): 978-981-4625-11-1
ISBN (ebook): 978-981-4625-12-8

Cover design by Cover Kitchen.

National Library Board, Singapore Cataloguing-in-Publication Data
Ismail, Barbara.
Spirit tiger /¬ Barbara Ismail. – First edition. – Singapore :¬ Monsoon
Books Pte Ltd,¬ 2015.
Pages ; cm. – (Kain songket mysteries ; volume III)
ISBN : 978-981-4625-11-1 (paperback)
1. Murder – Fiction. 2. Women detectives – Fiction. 3. Kelantan –
History – 20th century. II. Title.
PS3609
813.6 -- dc23      OCN898225221

Printed in Singapore
17  16  15                    1  2  3  4  5

For Wan Hamidah Wan Nawang and Abdul Malek Jusoh

## Acknowledgements

Thanks to Bonnie Tessler for suggesting the mechanics of a murder: no one looking at her would ever guess she'd do it so well! Puteh Shaharizan Shaari, Shahmim Dhilawala and Ashikin Mohd Ali Flindall were, as always, very helpful and encouraging. Zdena Nemeckova and Valerie Vogel read the drafts without complaint, and Eileen Alterbaum remains doubtful. Michele Andre was, and is, unflaggingly interested, and Mary Murphy ever supportive. Richard Lord deserves thanks as a peerless editor, and Philip Tatham as a peerless publisher. Without Doug Raybeck's teaching and mentoring, I never would have been able to do any of this. And my daughters, Jerushah and Arielle, are just wonderful, and truly make life worth living.

# Malay Glossary

*Abang*: Older Brother, a term of respect for someone somewhat older than you are. May also be used as a term of respect to a man roughly your same age.

*Adik*: Younger sibling.

*Air Halia*: Ginger Water, often served hot as an alternative to tea and rumored to enhance male ardor.

*Alamak*: An expression of surprise.

*Azimat*: Talisman, charm.

*Batik*: A wax print fabric, commonly used for women's sarong.

*Baju Melayu*: 'Malay Shirt': a man's traditional dress outfit, consisting of a high-necked shirt and loose pants, both usually in the same colour.

*Bersanding*: Sitting in state at a Malay wedding.

*Bongsu*: Youngest.

*Borek*: Speckled.

*Bomoh*: Curer, healer, magician.

*Budu*: Kelantanese fermented fish sauce.

*Che*: Mister.

*Cik*: Miss.

*Hala*: Tiger spirit.

*Hilir*: Downriver.

*Intan*: Diamond (a term of endearment).

*Jampi*: Magic spell.

*Jangan susah susah*: Don't trouble yourself.

*Jinn*: Spirits, demons.

*Kain Selamping*: A waistcloth worn with a baju melayu, folded around the waist and coming to mid-thigh, the dressier ones made of kain songket.

*Kain Songket*: The premier fabric of Kelantan, made of silk woven with geometric designs in gold thread. It is often used for wedding wear.

*Kakak*: Older sister (though not always literally).

*Kaki Ayam*: 'Chicken feet', i.e., barefoot.

*Kampong*: Village.

*Kasar*: Coarse, unrefined (of character).

*Kasehan*: A pity.

*Kempunan*: An intense longing, which can lead to illness if unfulfilled.

*Keropok*: Fish crackers which are fried before serving. In some areas of Malaysia, they are more often made of shrimp.

*Kueh*: Malay cakes, usually made with rice flour.

*Laksa*: A dish made with noodles in a thick coconut and fish broth, seasoned with a variety of herbs and spices. It is popular throughout Malaysia, and the Kelantan version is particularly rich and sweet.

*Maghrib*: Prayer at dusk.

*Main Puteri*: 'Princess Play', a spirit exorcism ceremony.

*Mak Andam*: Wedding expert.

*Mak Cik*: Auntie, a polite form of address for a middle-aged woman.

*Manja*: Spoiled, indulged.

*Merbau*: Zebra dove.

*Nenek*: Grandmother.

*Orang Luar*: Foreigners (outside person) from outside Kelantan.

*Pasar Besar*: Main Market.

*Pelisit*: A spirit familiar, often 'owned' by someone who feeds it and sends it out to bring back wealth or attack enemies.

*Pondok Polis*: Police 'hut', a small police station in a village.

*Sarong*: A tubular skirt of cotton fabric covering the wearer from waist to ankle.

*Sayang*: Darling.

*Serambi*: Verandah.

*Subuh*: The first prayer of the day, at dawn.

*Talak*: Pronouncement of divorce. After three *talak* (and they are cumulative) the divorce is final, and the couple can only remarry after the woman has married (and presumably divorced) another man.

*Tikar*: Sleeping mat, usually made of woven palm leaves.

*Ulu*: Upriver.

# Malay Idioms

*Asal terbang, burung lah*

Anything that flies is a bird: one who is easily pleased.

*Bagai punggok merindukan bulan*

Like an owl pining for the moon: to be lovesick.

*Berapa tingginya terbang bangau, akhirnya hinggap dibelakang kerbau juga*

No matter how high the padi bird flies, it ends up on a water buffalo's back: You cannot escape your origins, or your tastes.

*Bingong tengkat, cerdik begar*

When stupid, quarrelsome, when smart, difficult: said of someone difficult to control.

*Hidup segan, mati tak mahu*

Reluctant to live, unwilling to die: to be listless, aimless, indecisive.

*Hitam bagai pantat belanga*

As black as the bottom of a cooking pot.

*Kalah jadi abu, menang jadi arang*

Lose and become dust, win and become charcoal: there's no way to win.

*Kerana pijat mati tuma*

The louse dies because of the bug: to suffer because of the company you keep.

*Kerbau cucuk hidung*

A water buffalo with a ring through its nose: someone easily led.

*Kukur apa kepada kukur? Nyiur juga yang binasa*

What does rasping matter to the rasp? It's the coconut which suffers: It is all very well for you to say, but try it for yourself.

*Kurang ajar*

Insufficiently taught, not well brought up.

*Ludah mati pak, telan mati mak*

Spit it out and your father dies, swallow it and your mother dies: having no good options available to you.

*Mabok tahi telinga*

Dazed by talk.

*Macam pacat melompat*

Like a jumping leech: someone who drains you of everything you own.

*Nasi dimakan berasa lilin*

The rice that is eaten tastes like wax: to be lovesick.

*Panas se-tahun dihapuskan di hujan sehari*

A year of dry weather ruined by one day of rain: spoiling a lifetime of good reputation by one possibly minor misdeed.

*Pandai buat, tak pandai pera*

Good at making (children), not so good at taking care of them.

*Rusa dijumpa tak ada dikejar*

To find a deer without hunting it: to have something fall into your lap.

*Seperti apong di permain gelombang*

Like driftwood, a sport of the waves: Living aimlessly, a person of no account.

*Seperti kapas dimakan api*

Like cotton eaten by fire: completely and utterly destroyed.

*Seperti pinang se belah dua*

Like two halves of a betel nut: perfectly matched.

*Tanak dalam periok*

Cook rice in a rice pot: do things in the correct manner.

*Tinggal kelopak salak*

Only the salak (a fruit) wrapper is left: to be utterly destitute.

# Chapter I

There was no moon, but Yusuf knew his way well enough along the banks of the river to forego its light without compromising his balance. Besides, lights came through the cracks of the doors of the Chinese shophouses he walked behind, and with them the sounds of the interminable mah jongg games within.

Yusuf knew something about the economics of gambling, running a gambling parlour himself in the front rooms of his house, but the majority of his clientele were Malay rather than Chinese, and cards rather than mah jongg were the games of choice. Still, he was, as always, buoyed by the sounds of tiles smacking the tables and what was clearly the crowing of a triumphal win, even though it was in Hokkien, a Chinese dialect he didn't understand. The tone was clear enough without a translation.

Though gambling was frowned upon by the religious authorities in particular, and many Kelantanese in general, it nevertheless remained popular with a certain crowd, and Yusuf's place was never empty. Two years earlier, he'd even hired a waitress to take some of the pressure off his wife, who handled both the cooking and serving, and the availability of their meals allowed some of his more devoted customers to spend several uninterrupted days at Yusuf's tables. Liquor was also served—a great deal of it, since it was the ideal lubricant to keep gamblers playing. As alcohol was forbidden in Kelantan, it was presented in teacups, which preserved propriety.

Yusuf had been providing what he considered a valuable service to Kelantan for over twenty years, having opened his place immediately after his parents' death, when he inherited their home. He'd been a player long enough to know no gambler really enjoyed having to trek to the tables, wasting time and money on the journey. (Travelling all the way to Sungei Golok in order to find a game had taught him that.) What was needed, what would be greatly appreciated, would be an intimate and convenient spot close to home, providing home-cooked food in a familiar yet discreet location. Yusuf strove to offer this environment to his customers, and they flocked to it, as he knew they would.

He was a large man, in his fifties, bald but with a fringe of pepper-and-salt hair around the back of his head. He had small, shrewd eyes and a broad nose, made broader by the amount of whiskey he sipped throughout the day and into the night. He was big enough to serve as his own bouncer, and it was not only a matter of strength, but of skill which kept unhappy losers or overexcited drinkers from ignoring his orders more than once. He ran a quiet shop, wishing for no trouble from the neighbours, or – heaven forbid – the police. He correctly calculated that people might ignore what took place in his house if they didn't hear it:

once they did, however, they'd object.

One of his regulars, Ruslan, had an unfortunate run of luck at the tables, and had availed himself of house credit to rack up a spectacular loss. Yusuf had known him for years, and had no intention of letting the debt ride for too long, lest it become unmanageable. One evening, he appeared, genially, at Ruslan's house on Jalan Tengku Cik, letting his bulk loom over Ruslan and his nervous wife, Munira. He spoke on a variety of topics, including current events and the fortunes of Kelantan's football team (things were looking good after a win against Terengganu!), allowing his hosts' palpable anxiety to grow. He noted Munira twisting the side of her sarong, and the ever-so-slight shaking of her husband's hands against his coffee cup. Yusuf leaned back in his chair and smiled amiably, including both husband and wife in the smile's warmth. Then – still friendly, still calm – he introduced the topic of debt. There was no doubt in his listeners' minds, however, that the next talk might be far less friendly, and may well have included some unwelcome physical attention.

Ruslan was not a large man: he was rather rabbity and easily intimidated, and Yusuf did not believe he would be able to stand for long against a determined beating. As was his habit, Yusuf uttered no direct threats, and made no motion to touch his hosts in any way on this, his first visit. Rather, he allowed his debtor's imagination to do much of his work for him. He stressed the necessity of working things out, as though he might welcome any suggestion on their part as to how this might be done. He assured them, solicitously, that he would return to hear what they might have to say in two days' time. And with that, he politely took his leave, secure in the knowledge that his message had been received.

As large as he was, Yusuf moved gracefully and quickly along the muddy bank, taking a shortcut between Jalan Tengku Cik and his home near Kota Bharu's small Chinatown, next to the river. He walked behind the stalls of the Taman Sekebun Bunga, still serving late dinners at this hour, and the closed, silent stores next door. As he passed the shophouses, nearing his own home, he suddenly slipped on the mud, surprising himself. He stamped his feet and brushed off non-existent dust from his *sarong*, looking around to see what, if anything, might have caused him to nearly lose his balance. Seeing nothing, he shrugged, and turned to climb the low bank separating the river from the road.

As he reached the top, someone or something grabbed his shoulder and pulled him back, throwing him on his back into the river. It was shallow at the side, not too much more than wet mud, but the determined foot which now pressed into his chest knocked the air out of him, and within moments, his head was under only inches of water, but it was more than enough. After he stopped struggling, he was pushed out towards the middle of the river, where he joined the current and sank.

The ferry between Kota Bharu and Kampong Laut was a large, flat raft, capable of moving people, small livestock and motorbikes. It plied the Kelantan River from sun-up to sundown during the dry season, and somewhat more unpredictably during the monsoon. Whenever it went, however, it was almost always uneventful, and a good ferryman could, after a while, do it in his sleep, and many appeared to do just that.

On this particular trip, Awang the ferryman poled mechanically across the river, thinking of nothing in particular, squinting against the sun itself and its reflected rays on the muddy water. It was hot, but when wasn't it? He leaned hard against his pole, propelling the ferry and its passengers – including several tethered goats – toward Kota Bharu, when it seemed to hit something large and heavy, though only for a second, and he wondered whether he had imagined it.

He leaned over the side to get a better view through the murky water, not with any great interest, but nothing else was occupying him at the moment. He thought he saw something tumbling under the water, but it was hard to tell, and not until it suddenly appeared at the surface did he realize it was a man, and he'd been in the river for a while.

The police had been summoned by a nearly incoherent Awang, who might otherwise have been grateful for a diversion – but not for this one. He cried out when he realized what he had caught, and all his passengers rushed over to look, nearly capsizing the ferry in the melee. Shuddering, he brought the ferry to the shore as quickly as he could, and fled to the nearest *pondok polis*, breathlessly informing them of the body he'd swiped in the water. The two policeman exchanged a long, thoughtful look, and then as one decided to call Police Chief Osman, in Kota Bharu, who had handled murder before and would undoubtedly know what to do.

Osman had come to Kota Bharu from his home state of Perak, on the west coast of Malaysia, and had been unprepared for how different the east coast, and Kelantan especially, was compared to what he was accustomed to. The dialect, with its generous helping of Thai, dropped the letter 's', and its obscure vocabulary eluded him, though he tried manfully to master it. He still found it difficult to interview suspects or witnesses entirely in Kelantanese, and it sometimes seemed to him they spoke it more deeply just to show him up. He was, however, determined to do his best in the job, protecting life and limb in Kota Bharu and if necessary, the Kelantanese from themselves.

Osman arrived reluctantly: murder was a rare occurrence in Kelantan, a primarily rural state, yet this was the third time in as many years he'd been called to a crime scene to find a body, and he was feeling vaguely responsible for it.

The local police had, thankfully, gone back with Awang and brought the body back to shore, where it now lay on a wet sarong on the ground in front of the pondok, just downriver from the Chinese shophouses. Osman dropped to one knee for a closer look at it: it was, he thought, a mess. Waterlogged, perhaps nibbled upon by fish, it was bloated and disfigured, and he was glad no family members were there to see it. The police doctor placed a hand on the dead man's arm, and with a moue of distaste, turned him over. 'Does anyone know who he is?' he asked.

Rahman, Osman's right-hand man and invaluable interpreter, frowned. 'I've sent some officers to ask house to house,' he said, eyeing the corpse with caution. 'It looks as though he might not have travelled too far downriver,' he said, pointing to some weeds wrapped around his leg, 'We'd be lucky if that were true and he can be identified here. If he's from the *ulu,* it'll be more difficult.'

'We'll wait and see,' Osman said firmly.

They did not have long to wait. A short, very dark woman was walking in step with one of the officers, looking both wary and fascinated. She came closer to the body, then stood on tiptoe and peered over at it. She nodded slowly. '*Cik* Yusuf,' she said with finality.

No one had been looking for Yusuf, though no one remembered seeing him for over three days. Each person who might have been expected to notice he was gone merely assumed he was elsewhere: his was that kind of life. His wife thought he might have gone to Sungei Golok, across the border in Thailand, to bring back a supply of whiskey. His children gave little thought to his absences since they were both common and unexplained. And his clients … well, they had other things on their minds.

And now it appeared he'd been fished out of the Kelantan River, waterlogged and bedraggled, clearly having been in it for several days.

# Chapter II

Puteh was tired. It had been a long morning, with all seven of her young children whining for attention and food, and she hadn't quite enough of either for them. Money was always tight: she'd grown up with that state, so working within those parameters was no surprise to her. Children seemed to keep coming, even though she privately felt they already had more than enough. A lifelong habit of keeping bad news to herself kept her from discussing this with her husband, though she doubted he'd be much interested even if she broached the subject with him.

She'd been married off early, at fifteen, to a man ten years older than she was, and whom she had never met. However, her parents, overburdened with plenty of younger children of their own and a perennial shortage of funds, thought it might benefit Puteh as well as them to have someone else provide for her.

Sadly, their choice had been a poor one. Suleiman was a good-natured man, but not a strong one, and temptations of all kinds seemed to ensnare him with ease. He greeted gambling, drinking, and carousing with friends with far more enthusiasm than any domestic responsibilities. '*Pandai buat, tak pandai pera,*' people said of him: good at making children, not so much in taking care of them.

As usual, Suleiman was out, though where, Puteh could not say. Nor did she care actually; if he wasn't at home, helping her, or possibly out taking an odd job to pay the rent, it didn't matter to her where he'd gone. All the work in the house would fall to her anyway, and his actual whereabouts did nothing to change that. Sighing deeply, she began to sort the clothes in her basket in preparation for washing them.

She sat on a rock beside the river, slowly picking out each piece, deliberately laying them in small, separate piles. She hoped to take as much time as possible in her task. One of her neighbours was watching the children, and she treasured her short break from their demands.

She picked up a pair of Suleiman's pants, noting faint mud stains along the bottom hem, and as she tossed them to one side, she thought she heard a crinkle. She retrieved them and checked through the pockets, pulling out a crumpled ball of thin paper. She was about to throw it away, when she noticed what appeared to be Arabic script along one side: curious, she smoothed it against her knee and squinted at it. She read slowly, shaping the words with her lips as she read, then glancing up and staring across the river at Kampong Laut, not registering anything she saw there.

She could not credit what she had read and, in a few moments, turned back to the document and read it again, expecting it to change its meaning into something she could better digest. But the next reading remained the same, as did the third. She turned blindly from her laundry, and still clutching the crushed paper, stumbled back towards her house. She'd been divorced.

'How could you?' she asked him, noting in her mind how trite it sounded, even to her, but unable to come up with any other question she wanted answered. He'd come home in the afternoon – just as though nothing had happened – looking for dinner and a nap and clean clothes, as always. But now she knew she'd been divorced for over a week and he hadn't bothered to tell her. How could he, indeed?

Suleiman did not appear to have an answer prepared, or even considered. He kept opening and closing his mouth, as though planning to speak, though he could not. Puteh could not decide whether to cry or slap him, and it seemed like an endless amount of time went by before he could finally choked out, 'What?'

Not the most eloquent excuse, but it was all she had to work with. 'I found it,' she said calmly, waving the decree in front of his face. 'Your divorce. Last week?' She reminded him. He remained at a loss.

'Well,' he finally began, looking furtively around the room as though there might be someone in the corner who might help him, 'it's true.' He stammered slightly. 'But I didn't think ...'

She waited to hear what he didn't think, and for a while nothing seemed forthcoming. 'I mean,' he amended, 'it wasn't my idea.' He looked at her, cocking his head. 'It was her idea,' he further detailed. 'She wanted to get married, but I didn't really. And it's only one *talak*,' he explained helpfully, 'so nothing is permanent.'

'Who is she?'

He looked abashed. 'You know *Che* Yusuf's place? Where I sometimes play cards?'

More than sometimes: she often suspected Yusuf's front room was Suleiman's real home. 'She helps there.' He looked even more uncomfortable. 'The waitress? Khatijah?'

He nodded reluctantly. It was now Puteh's turn to be struck dumb. Khatijah was small and dark-skinned and a touch haggard, as befitted a waitress in a gambling den. She had been long divorced and childless, though Puteh heard she had recently adopted a child: a Chinese girl whose parents were willing to part with her. It now clicked.

'And you are to be the father to her new child? You've already got seven here! You don't pay any attention to them!' She looked around at her brood, the eldest of whom was following the conversation like a ping pong match, the youngest of whom could not yet crawl. She turned her attention back to Suleiman, suddenly no longer bereft about the divorce, but fed up: with his gambling, with his disinterest in family life, and now with his secret divorce. She grabbed her small purse with her emergency money – a completely insignificant amount – and walked out, leaving Suleiman to cope with his children.

She stood in front of her house for a moment, regarding it as she rarely did, from the outside, dispassionately. It was at the far end of Kampong Penambang, closest to Kota Bharu, and assuredly one of the least impressive houses in the area. Unpainted, with just the slightest lean, it looked exhausted, much as she felt. The roof needed repair, the tiny front porch was rickety, and from here, she wondered how she allowed any of the children to play on it when it looked as though it might collapse at the slightest pressure. At least the yard was swept.

She stood irresolutely, unable to decide where to go in her new-found freedom. She began walking towards the middle of Kampong Penambang, towards the main road and the large *Kain Songket* emporia which lined it. She'd thought about going into one, running her hands over the fine fabric and think about buying it, but she hadn't been able to with her small army of children in tow. Now, however, it was her time, and she picked up her pace as she approached the imposing, pillared shops filled with *songket*.

She entered cautiously, ever mindful of the fact she did not possess even a small fraction of the money needed to buy any of these fabrics. She shyly kept her eyes down, not wanting to draw the attention of any salespeople. She ran her hand slowly and lightly over the wedding fabrics arrayed on a table, thrilled to feel the raised pattern, admiring the play of the light on the gold thread.

'He's dead, you know,' one salesgirl whispered to another. 'They found him in the river, and they said he'd been there for days.' She nodded at her friend, who shuddered. 'What must he have looked like by then?' she asked. 'With the fish and everything.'

'Horrible,' stated the first. 'It's terrible.'

Puteh did not lift her head, but moved towards them, the better to listen.

'But you know, gambling and all that,' the first continued. 'Is it surprising? My father says it's a judgement on him.'

The other nodded. 'Yes, but drowning? Who would have done it?'

'There are probably lots of people who would have wanted to,' she said briskly. 'But I feel sorry for his family.'

As another customer walked in, they abandoned their conversation, but Puteh had gone cold. She turned and left the shop, the thrill of the fabrics dissipated. Feeling trapped, unable to see her way out of her situation, she trudged back to her house to once again pick up the responsibilities she left there not more than fifteen minutes ago. Her neighbour Rubiah fell into step next to her on the road. Rubiah was Puteh's mother's age, and part of a two-woman team celebrated for solving murders in Kelantan. She was also, by her own blushing admission, the premier Malay cake chef in Kelantan.

Rubiah had lived in Kampong Penambang all her life and knew Puteh's family from childhood. She saw and understood the problems in Puteh's marriage, and pitied her, trying to help whenever it was possible. 'Did you hear about *Che* Yusuf?' she asked.

'Yusuf?' Puteh stammered. Was it Yusuf they found?

Rubiah nodded. 'You know,' she said kindly, aware of just how well Puteh did know, 'the one who has gambling at his house.'

'What?' Puteh was wide-eyed.

'He died,' Rubiah told her flatly. 'They just pulled him out of the river. He drowned, it seems. A couple of days ago.'

Puteh stared at the ground, concentrating on putting one foot in front of the other. Rubiah put her hand on her shoulder. 'I don't know if that means there won't be any more games, or whether *Cik* Noriah will keep it open. I mean, it isn't open now. *Cik* Noriah's just found out it was Yusuf they brought out of the river, so she's preparing for the funeral now.'

Puteh nodded, not trusting herself to speak. Rubiah watched her with concern. 'Are you alright, Puteh?'

She bit her lip, trying to keep herself silent. 'I'm glad,' she burst out between clenched teeth, 'I'm glad he's dead. Maybe it will save some other people from this kind of life.' And she burst into tears.

# Chapter III

Mamat sat on the front porch, under the protection of the roof, in the cool of the late afternoon. The sun slanted through the fruit trees in the yard and the coconut and betel palms scattered throughout the *kampong*, but it no longer burned. Carefully surrounding him were rattan bird cages housing his treasured flock of *merbok* – zebra doves, famed for their song. Like many Kelantan avian aficionados, Mamat fussed over his birds, devised special diets and developed theories concerning the right ratio of sun to shade in which they could rest. His regimen was flexible, and often changed, though his devotion and attention had never flagged in all the years his wife, Maryam, had known him. She shared his delight in the birds, and often assisted in cosseting them, mashing their bananas with more exotic ingredients and feeding them from her own fingers.

Tonight's meal was even more exotic than usual, in preparation for a singing competition to be held in a field near Kubang Kerian – the birds were now in serious training! Mamat mixed the finest of grains with bananas and a touch of honey to sweeten their song and soothe their throats. He had been toying with the idea of adding papaya to the mix, which another bird fancier told him helped their stamina and their mood so they were more inclined to sing. Now was the time to act, he believed, and with great personal fanfare, he included ripe papaya, and even the slightest touch of ginger to the gruel. He fed the birds directly from his hands, and watched them closely for signs of immediate improvement in strength and confidence. He thought he may have glimpsed it, but could not really be certain.

Maryam emerged from the house onto the porch, having completed most of the preparations for dinner and leaving the finishing touches in the hands of her high school-aged daughter, Aliza. Aliza was more than capable of handling dinner, and much else besides. She was taking her O-level exams and planned to become a teacher. Her family agreed it was an excellent choice and that she would be a formidable teacher, able to quell an unruly class in one freezing glance. She practiced such glances on her younger brother, Yi, who, to his mother's surprise, was often quelled by them.

While Aliza organized the kitchen and ran herd over Yi, Maryam made herself comfortable sitting on the top step to the porch, extracting a hand-rolled cigarette from the folds of her sarong.

'Don't get any smoke near the birds,' warned Mamat. 'I don't want it affecting their song.'

Maryam mildly agreed and turned her head slightly away from the cages. She had a pretty, pleasant face with large brown eyes, a snub nose and thick, dark hair, which she wore in a no-

nonsense bun. She was a cheerful, middle-aged Malay woman, a *Mak Cik,* of the sorority which ruled Kelantan both socially and economically, and Maryam participated in both fields of endeavour. She owned a stall in Kota Bharu's main market, the epicentre of the state's flourishing mercantile activity, in which she sold *kain songket* cloth made in Kampong Penambang itself. She held herself as one aware of her own value. As indeed she was, with reason to be proud of the living she provided for her family, and her place in Kelantanese society.

Sitting on the porch with her husband and their birds, with sounds of determined activity coming from the kitchen, Maryam radiated contentment. There were no clouds on her emotional horizon. Her oldest son Azmi was soon to be married; her married daughter, Ashikin was now expecting her second child; Aliza, who had been badly hurt during a crime investigation not long before, was not only recovered, but was studying hard for her exams and would no doubt be marvelously successful. And Yi, her youngest, was at least staying out of trouble and doing tolerably well at school. What more could a mother ask for?

She looked forward to the bird singing competition coming up in a week. Though Maryam herself did not gamble, and Mamat would only make a small bet to show his confidence in his birds, thousands of ringgit changed hands during these contests, and the winning birds were often sold for mind-boggling sums. Their birds had not yet ever won a major event, but had been reliably successful in neighbourhood gatherings, and Mamat was now grooming them for the big time.

Kelantan was a centre for all manner of intra-animal competitions. There was cock fighting, with trained roosters equipped with razors attached to their legs; bull fighting involving two bulls trying to drive each other out of the ring; and even Siamese fighting fish tournaments. All of these attracted their own circle of experts, with a distinct corpus of expertise: magic, breeding, grooming and feeding. Men – for it was always they – devoted the vast majority of their time to their chosen pursuit, devising diets, positioning and training regimens for their animals.

Singing contests were held in large, dry fields, with tall poles arranged in a circle. Birds preferred to be in high places when they sang, and therefore each bird in its cage was run up the pole to hang twelve feet or more off the ground, where they could give full-throated energy to their song. The judge would stroll from one pole to another listening to each bird and award prizes based on the sweetness and length of the song.

Opinion differed widely on the best position to get for the birds; did they prefer facing north or south? Most competitions were held in the morning, before the real heat of the day set in. Therefore, did the birds prefer to look toward the east, or were they happier facing away from the sun? And since their rattan cages were opened on all sides, did this really matter, since the birds could turn to face whichever direction they preferred. Or did they generally sit only on their perches, refusing to experiment? Bird behavior often changed from one event to the next, and even the least adventuresome creatures might surprise their owners.

Mamat was thrumming with anxiety about this tournament.

Of all his birds, he believed one called Borek, Speckled, to be the most likely to come home with honours. He was his favourite bird – a plump, speckled (of course) dove with an attentive expression and a winning way of cocking his head when regarding Mamat. Maryam was vastly amused by Mamat's clear belief that Borek understood Malay and cocked his head at him because he wondered what he would say next. Maryam was fond of the birds, but was under no illusions that they understood her, or yearned for a more intimate connection.

Mamat had always spent hours with Ah Pak, a Chinese store owner and respected *merbok* expert. It was Ah Pak who suggested the touch of ginger to the birds' food, explaining that it would 'jolt' the birds into singing more enthusiastically than they had ever done before, and it was he who gave Mamat tips on the best placement of birds at a tournament.

Though he ostensibly sold motorcycle parts, and, in fact, those parts littered the small, dark front room of his shop which opened up onto the sidewalk, his real and abiding passion was songbirds. Cages of his latest acquisitions, some of whom had been bought in Thailand for more money than Mamat had ever in his whole life seen in one place, hung on the walls, up high where the birds might be inspired to sing. Conversation at Ah Pak's covered almost nothing other than birds, and groups of men, with little else in common, could spend hours immersed in discussion, communing on a deep and satisfying level.

Ah Pak's great-grandfather came to Kelantan from Fukien, and settled in the Kota Bharu area, marrying a local Chinese girl. He began trading in farming implements, opening a tiny store next to the Kelantan River among the small group of other Chinese, and there he raised a large family. His daughters married men from Gua Musang, far in the southern jungle, which was a primarily Chinese town; his sons stayed with him in Kota Bharu and helped with the business.

Ah Pak's father branched into motorcycle and car parts immediately after the war, foreseeing a demand for the ability to travel, to join the modern world. Though Ah Pak dutifully followed him, his real passion lay elsewhere, in gambling in general and song birds in particular. He made money from his motorcycle parts business, but his heart wasn't in it, and had never been. He began as a boy playing mah jongg – and winning. He was an excellent player with a phenomenal memory, which also served him in good stead when he experimented with card games and dice.

As he matured, he looked for something to engage his intellect as well as his adrenaline, and he turned to the raising of *merbok* for competition. He began with one dove, which he coddled and raised, expanding gradually into several more, and then, after consulting older, more experienced owners and trainers, he began experimenting with his own theories on what made birds sing well.

Ah Pak was a small man, shorter than Mamat and considerably more round. His hair was thick and bristly, cut in a way which left it standing straight up from his head, and he often ran his hands through it and vigorously scratched his scalp while thinking. He had a wide and friendly face, with a broad nose, high cheekbones and small, wide-set eyes. He smiled often, giggled when amused (which was also often), and rarely if ever lost his temper. Most days, Ah Pak could be found in his usual work uniform, consisting of a sleeveless white undershirt; a muted green plaid cotton sarong, often hiked up between his legs in a modified loincloth; brown rubber flip-flops; and a toothpick sticking out the side of his mouth. He spoke perfect Kelantanese, having grown up on it, some standard Malay, basic English and Hokkien. He was, in short, the perfect, well-rounded Kota Bharu merchant.

Ah Pak's oldest son, Kit Siang, was only sixteen, but already followed his father's path. He, too, was a well-known gambler, first trying his luck locally at Yusuf's place together with his group of friends. As is often the case, young gamblers, inexperienced and naïve, lose big, and these boys were no exception. Yusuf knew well enough that Ah Pak could pay for his son's losses, and extended him generous house credit. Ah Pak took the first request for payment philosophically enough, feeling he was certainly in no position to lecture Kit Siang, who, after all, came by it honestly. However, after politely asking Yusuf not to extend any more credit, and to limit Kit Siang's losses to what was actually in his pocket, Ah Pak did not pay as happily the second time, and even less so the third. Reasoning with Kit Siang did no good, as Ah Pak expected, and finally an open rift developed between the two older men.

Ah Pak believed Yusuf took advantage of his good nature,

and mistook his low key geniality for a lack of determination, and indeed, in this respect, Yusuf clearly miscalculated. Not all gamblers were feckless and weak-willed, nor was Yusuf's size a guarantee of successful intimidation, even to those who looked most likely to be cowed by it.

# Chapter IV

With Yusuf gone, Noriah wasn't quite sure what to do. She had always served as her husband's lieutenant, ably and independently carrying out his direction, ensuring both home and business ran smoothly so he could devote himself to a higher calling, such as debt collection. But without him, things seemed muddy and uncertain. Gambling had ceased, of course – it would be most unseemly to continue it at a time like this. The tables were silent, the house closed. Relatives had gathered, bringing food with them and preparing it endlessly in her kitchen. Her children lounged on the couch and chairs in the living room, grieving, she hoped; sullen, she suspected.

The funeral had been held the day after the body was found, and while many people came, it seemed to Noriah not many really mourned, as she herself did not. The atmosphere was correct and almost businesslike, with the burial and reception at home going off without a hiccup. Yet she felt it lacked soul, and real feeling. She did not put her own inner calm down to shock, or the surprise of losing Yusuf so precipitously; rather, it was a shrugging off of something which had been fine in its day, and was now over. That realization made her far sadder than Yusuf's passing: shouldn't a wife and family feel more than a shrug and a sigh? Still, there was no use trying to deceive herself into believing she was more affected than she actually was, and anyway, she had plans to make regarding the future.

Noriah was a child of Kampong Penambang and had married Yusuf after divorcing her first husband, who had been chosen for her by her parents. She was a pretty girl with a winning smile, quick-thinking and vivacious. People always liked being around her because she was fun and rarely in other than a good mood.

That first husband was older than she was, and accustomed to giving orders and having them carried out with dispatch: after her first child was born, she decided that she could no longer provide the military precision he seemed to crave. She'd noted with admiration how Yusuf had turned his parents' house into a noteworthy source of income, and she liked a man with a bit of heft to him. He looked solid and dependable.

Yusuf, too, was recently divorced for the second time, and he, too, sought reliability above all else. In that they were perfectly matched: *seperti pinang se belah dua,* like two halves of a betel nut. Their coming together and almost immediate marriage were less a product of passion than of practicality and mutual requirements. Yusuf would provide for her, and act as a father to her infant son. She, in turn, would help him with the gambling hall, give him children, care for them, and pepper him with as few questions as possible. It worked to both their satisfactions for many years.

And yet. She wondered about his relationship with Khatijah, the dark waitress he'd hired to help Noriah with the chores around the tables. It was true she had a heavy work load, what with cooking dinners and serving them, in addition to everything else, but she hadn't complained or asked for any help, and Yusuf wasn't the kind of husband to anticipate her wants, particularly if they would cost him money.

Though she personally saw little attractive in Khatijah (who looked as though she'd had a hard life and bore all the marks of it), she had to admit their customers seemed to be drawn to her. Hadn't Suleiman actually married her? It still astonished her that he did, and that he'd divorced Puteh to do it. And if Khatijah could so ensnare Suleiman (though admittedly, he was no particular prize), could she not have worked some of her wiles on Yusuf himself?

Yusuf was not amused by her marriage to Suleiman, Noriah could see that. Their nuptials were a cause of high hilarity among Suleiman's fellow gamblers, and the night they actually did wed was an occasion for endless toasts and screaming, drunken laughter. Yusuf, she noted, kept apart from the celebration, his face a careful, expressionless mask. At the time, Noriah wondered why he would care, and see it as something bad, rather than what it was: a banner night for their liquor sales and heavier than usual losses on the part of their inebriated clientele. She wondered after that if he was jealous of Khatijah marrying another man, even one as useless as Suleiman.

One could never fathom men, and what they might find

attractive. After all, Puteh was much prettier than Khatijah, and almost certainly better natured, too. Khatijah was too small and thin and, yes, too dark for Noriah's taste. Kelantanese women were proud of their reputation for both beauty and fair skin, and Khatijah was a disgrace to Kelantan on both counts: *hitam bagai pantat belanga,* as black as the bottom of a cooking pot.

Though Khatijah ostensibly helped Noriah, and had always done as she had been ordered, Noriah sensed a silent insubordination in her, a metaphorical tossing of the hair when Noriah spoke to her. It was never obvious enough to discipline her, or even really mention it without providing a stage from which Khatijah could proclaim her innocence and claim to be persecuted, and Noriah was too smart to offer her that kind of opportunity.

For such a poor specimen, she already showed off far more often than warranted. Even yesterday, Khatijah preened herself on having identified Yusuf's body, as though it was a rare and precious skill she'd demonstrated, instead of merely having recognized her employer of two years after he died. And while Noriah didn't think anything had actually occurred between Yusuf and Khatijah (and she was not one to turn away from the truth because it was either inconvenient or unwelcome), she felt there was some kind of connection between them she didn't like.

Her first priority would be to get some help with the business. Her son was too young and, besides, she hoped for something better, more respectable, for him than running a gambling hall. She'd need someone capable of keeping order, and perhaps to help her collect debts. She was dismayed by the necessity of finding someone like this, as she would be forced to share the profit with him, and the longer their relationship continued, the larger share he'd probably want. She began to consider who she might approach: someone who could help her without wanting to take over. Someone not too bright.

# Chapter V

Maryam knew Yusuf and felt sorry for his family upon losing him, though it in no way implied she approved of turning a *kampong* house into a gambling parlour, or in providing space in which people could exercise the weakest parts of their characters. She was a realist, and no puritan, but she'd seen the pain Mamat's father had caused his young family with drinking and gambling, and how it had forced Mamat to grow up so soon. It was always those who could least afford to lose who seemed to gamble, she reflected, and it preyed on those who were damaged and therefore vulnerable. It had been a quiet place, however, and Maryam had been reluctant to get involved by reporting it to the police, and so she ignored it. (The police may have already known anyway.)

The whole *kampong* knew about the long-suffering Puteh, and her worthless husband, and how he had become even more worthless, if such a thing were possible, in divorcing her. Maryam pitied her: such a young woman thrust into such an impossible situation. She couldn't decide whether Puteh was better off married to Suleiman or divorced from him. Married, at least there was a possibility that someday he might bring home some money; divorced, perhaps she could meet someone else and, at least, what little money she could get her hands on wouldn't be thrown away on cards and liquor. All in all, she was inclined towards the side of divorce: maybe Puteh was luckier than she knew in getting rid of Suleiman, though it no doubt rankled to have lost him to such a specimen as Khatijah.

Maryam sat ruminating on her front porch, leaning against one of the posts, cataloguing her stock of *kain songket* and local batik made by her older brother, Malek. She sorted the *songket* by colour, so that she could easily reach for the right fabric when told the colour scheme for any particular wedding. It was early morning, and the sun had just come up, so it was still relatively cool. Maryam's cousin and best friend, Rubiah, sauntered over from her own home nearby, and comfortably deposited herself on the top step, unwrapping a bundle of newly baked cakes from her stock ready for market. Maryam leaned over to examine the merchandise, deliberately choosing two different cakes and eating them before speaking.

'What's new?'

Rubiah shook her head absentmindedly. 'Nothing.'

'Sad,' Maryam commented on Yusuf's funeral, which they had both attended the day before. 'Do you think Noriah will close it now?'

Rubiah considered this as though it had not previously occurred to her. 'I don't think she wants to. They make a lot of money from it.'

Maryam sniffed. 'It isn't a good way to do it. There are better ways.'

'I know. But they're used to this. I think she'll want to keep going if she can. Have you heard anything about the investigation?' she asked innocently.

Maryam gave her a sharp look. 'Not yet. But you know, I'm interested.'

Rubiah gasped. 'No!'

'Well, yes,' she admitted. 'You know, it seems that so many people might have a reason to want *Che* Yusuf ... out of the way,' she finished primly, unwilling to say 'dead'. 'All these gamblers, you know, already on the wrong path ...'

'So murder wouldn't be much of a stretch for them, is that what you mean?'

Maryam shrugged, and ran her hands over the pile of *songket* in front of her. '*Kerana pijat mati tuma',* she said finally – the louse dies because of the bug. 'He must have been killed because of the people he mixed with. That kind of company can't lead to anything good. No one,' she continued, warming to her topic, 'meets decent people while gambling like that. So it stands to reason, doesn't it, that one of them killed him. For running a place like that.' She seemed satisfied with her logic.

Rubiah did not look as though she entirely agreed, but said nothing for a moment. 'Has Osman been to see you?'

'Not yet,' Maryam said. 'But I expect him at any time.'

She was prophetic. Once she was ensconced in her stall in the market, centrally located in the fabric section on the ground floor – a truly premier site inherited from her mother – a hand-rolled cigarette, unlit, between her lips and several pieces of *songket* unfurled on the counter to be admired by the customer in front of her, Osman appeared.

He always looked diffident when he entered the market. For all the status of his position outside the market, in here he was at a disadvantage, being a man and a West Coast Malay and, most important, not a trader. He knew his only hope for a fair price was the pity of the seller, a disinclination to fleece an especially woolly sheep, and this irritated him. He wanted to be respected, not coddled like a child, but that was not about to happen within the confines of the *pasar besar*.

On this day, he moved sideways, crab-like, through the crowded aisles, followed by Rahman, who felt no such qualms or inferiority, since he had female relatives working here and was confident in their ability to protect him.

Maryam noticed him and smiled to herself with satisfaction. It was always uplifting to be proven right yet again. She turned that same pleased smile on her customer, who was somewhat surprised to see Maryam's face light up, though no deal had yet been made.

'Listen to me,' she advised the woman and her daughter in front of her, petting the pale pink *kain songket* like a favourite cat. 'I can see you love this fabric, of course, you do! Who wouldn't, with this kind of quality and the colour?

Well, it's perfect, I think we all agree, right?' She looked at them, seeking confirmation, which she received from the bride-to-be, though the mother kept a dour and disapproving face – no doubt in order to improve her bargaining position.

'It's lovely,' the girl said appreciatively, stroking the fabric with a shy smile.

'*Asal terbang, burung lah,*' her mother sniffed, 'Anything that flies is a bird to her. She's easily pleased,' she added disapprovingly. 'I'm not so sure …'

'About the colour?' Maryam asked with a polite smile. 'Because the quality is beyond doubt, there's no question about it. Look at these threads,' she urged, 'do you see how fine the silk is?'

She leaned to her side and lit her cigarette. She needed some kind of a break with this woman. She hoped this was put on for her benefit, and not her usual disposition, which would make her unbearable. She began wrapping the fabric in brown paper. She often found the assumption that a deal was immanent often made it so, and wrapping the merchandise as though the customer had already bought it seemed to make them also feel they'd agreed. This customer seemed more strong-minded than most.

'Why are you wrapping it?' she asked sharply. 'Have we agreed?'

'No?' Maryam asked mildly. 'I'm so sorry…' She began slowly, very slowly, unwrapping it, preparing to place it, regretfully, back on the counter.

'*Mak!*' The bride finally spoke up. '*Mak*, listen…'

Her mother led her away a few steps from the stall, no doubt to lecture her on not seeming to be too enthusiastic about any particular merchandise, and in so doing, they left some space in front of Maryam into which Osman slid.

'*Mak Cik*!' he greeted her happily.

'*Che* Osman!' she replied in the same mood. 'How nice to see you! I was just talking about you to *Mak Cik* Rubiah, you know, and I was telling her that I thought you might be coming to see me one of these days.'

Osman blushed, but not quite to the tips of his ears as he had routinely done before he was married. *His wife must be making him more mature*, she thought.

'I'd like your help,' Osman said diffidently. 'I know you don't want to be involved in police business again, like you said, but …'

Maryam interrupted him imperiously. 'This one is different,' she informed him. 'This one I want to know more about. You know, I think it's one of the gamblers he catered to. Can you be surprised? People like that, I mean, people who have already begun to waste their lives, it stands to reason they might be tempted to do all sorts of things. Right?' she prodded him.

He neither nodded nor shook his head, but instead moved it around aimlessly. It was a lame response, he knew, but he was unable to come up with anything else sufficiently placating while still expressing some level of doubt. 'Well,' he explained, 'we don't know yet if it's anyone from his … business,' for lack of another term, 'it still could be *anyone*.'

'Nonsense,' Maryam corrected him with asperity. 'Why waste time? It's one of those wastrels, and I'll be happy to find him. Help you find him,' she corrected herself politely. She began gathering up her fabrics and putting her money neatly away in the cardboard box she used as a cash register. 'Let's get Rubiah and start planning.'

She led him up the stairs to Rubiah's stall, where her cousin presided over an immense assortment of Kelantanese *kueh*, each of the cakes artistically arranged with an eye towards colour combinations and flow. She smiled as she saw Osman, and began picking out the most fattening collection of cakes for him, as part of her private goal of putting some weight on him. She looked up from the hillock of pastry she built and noticed Maryam's expression, and her own changed from pleasant anticipation to deep concern.

'You aren't,' she said to Maryam.

'I am,' Maryam said calmly. 'I want to see what these people are like.'

'Like anyone else,' Rubiah told her.

'I don't think so,' Maryam considered. 'There's something different about them, I think, that made them start gambling and all that,' she waved her hand to encompass drinking and loose women. 'I want to know.'

'You could get hurt again,' Rubiah argued.

Maryam dismissed this, as though no reprobate could possibly overpower her. 'Anyway, we're here to plan.' She looked closely at Osman, applying himself diligently to the cakes before him. 'I hear the gambling is closed down now, after Yusuf's death. I think the best think to do it talk to Noriah, and find out who were the customers, and then go talk to them.'

'You think they'll confess immediately?' Rubiah asked sarcastically.

'Probably not.' Maryam refused to be baited. 'It might take some time.' She turned to Osman. 'Will Rahman come?' He nodded. 'Azrina?' This was Osman's wife, relatively new in Kelantan, who'd just begun teaching math at the Sultanah Zainab School. She was a crime fiction fan, who, Maryam could see, itched to try her hand at detecting. Maryam thought she'd be good at it, too, since she was smart and tenacious. She was sure Azrina had already tamed Osman (that would have taken only a short time) and was now ready for some real work.

Osman looked startled, and then thoughtful. 'I don't know,' he said slowly. 'I mean, she's a math teacher…'

'And I'm a cloth seller,' Maryam reminded him. 'What does that mean?'

He considered what to say. It's too dangerous for my *wife*? That would go down badly. And Azrina's ability to understand Kelantanese, though not to speak it, was improving far beyond his. And most important, he could not possibly stop her if she made up her mind to do it.

# Chapter VI

Noriah and Yusuf lived not too far from the family home they used for gambling. It was in a large and airy *kampong* house with a wide covered porch, convenient for lounging while avoiding the direct glare of the sun; a large front room complete with television; sofa and loveseat; and bedrooms and kitchen behind. It was freshly painted and beautifully kept, quite near the main road running from Kota Bharu to Pantai Cinta Berahi, through Kampong Penambang.

Mariam and Rubiah had known Noriah for years as a neighbour, albeit a slightly disreputable one, and went to her house bearing both cakes and *laksa*, as befitted a call on a recently bereaved family. Dressed in their everyday clothing, calling in the middle of the morning, it was as informal an event as they could contrive. (Rubiah's two daughters were drafted to mind both of their stalls for a few hours – how much damage could they do? Maryam didn't like to think about it.)

Noriah, no fool at all, immediately understood why they had come and therefore dispensed with preliminary chitchat and got right down to the business of naming anyone she considered a suspect. However businesslike this discussion would be, it could not flow in an easy and unrestricted way without sufficient coffee, cake and cigarettes to ensure the participants were fully at their ease. All refreshments were served outside in generous quantities, and after their arrival, the three *Mak Ciks* with one goal in mind began to talk.

'It's a good theory,' Noriah said approvingly upon hearing Maryam's thoughts on the probable killer. 'Of course, someone who was often in our shop would have known Yusuf best and I hear that most murders are committed by people who know the victim, right?'

Maryam nodded sagely. Who else?

'First,' Noriah continued briskly, as though in a business meeting, 'we should look at people who owed Yusuf money. There always are where people are playing cards and things, but Yusuf always managed it quite well. He never let it get out of hand. There's Ruslan, of course. He owed, well …' she thought for a moment, 'He still owes quite a bit, and he still hasn't paid. Of course, with all that's happened, I naturally forgot about it,' she inclined her head slightly, a gesture encompassing the funeral and all that caused it, 'But Yusuf said he would be calling on him to discuss it. I don't know if he already had or not.'

'By discuss, you mean …?' Maryam asked delicately.

'Oh no,' Noriah corrected her amiably, no offense taken. 'Just discuss. At least at first,' she added in the interest of full disclosure. 'But I don't think anything had gone that far with Ruslan.' Maryam nodded again, not wanting to make apparent how little she knew about what going that far entailed. But she could guess.

'Then Zainuddin,' she counted on her fingers. Maryam and Rubiah did not recognize the name: someone from Kota Bharu, then. 'He's owed for a while, paying off little by little. I don't like him,' she said bluntly, 'and I told Yusuf he shouldn't let him gamble here. He was too *kasar* for us here, no manners at all.' What did it take, Maryam wondered, to be considered too *kasar* for a low-down gambling den? Zainuddin, unseen, shot to the top of her suspect list.

'Do you know where all these people live?' Maryam asked.

Noriah nodded vaguely. 'I have to look in Yusuf's notebooks, but I'm sure he has some notes in there. They should be easy to find: no one came here from that far away.' She searched her memory again. She looked hard and Maryam and sighed, then continued.

'There's another. I don't really know what to say about it, except that something was going on. Khatijah. You know her.' They did, and apparently all three shared the same opinion about her. 'Yusuf was watching her. He was interested in her. I don't know if it was that way,' she explained, seeing the look they exchanged. 'Of course, that kind of thing always occurs to me first, too, but I'm not sure that was it. But something.

'The night she married Suleiman, there was a celebration here: drinking and so on.' She looked prim, as though she, too, deeply disapproved. Maryam discounted it immediately as window dressing for the neighbours.

'And, of course, Khatijah was in the middle of it, and Yusuf wasn't really happy at all, or having a good time with his customers. He was looking at her, watching her.'

'Was he jealous?' It seemed amazing even as she asked it. 'I mean, of Suleiman?' This seemed even more improbable.

Clearly, Noriah agreed. She smirked, and nearly laughed. 'I can't imagine. Jealous of Suleiman! That poor man, no backbone at all. No, I can't imagine that. Anyway,' she said cattily, though accurately, 'who else would marry Khatijah?'

'True enough,' Maryam responded, 'but I'm not sure that does much to help Puteh.'

'Ah, Puteh. *Kasehan.* She might be better off without him,' Noriah said, echoing Maryam's previous musings. 'I don't think he's ever going to pull himself together, he's weak,' Noriah dismissed him. 'Still, I feel sorry for her: *kalah jadi abu, menang jadi arang,* lose and you're dust, win and you're charcoal. With Suleiman, she can't win, divorced or married, I'm afraid.'

'She knows about his marrying Khatijah,' Rubiah stated. 'She found the *talak* in his pants pocket when she washed them.'

'*Alamak!*' exclaimed Noriah. 'He didn't!'

Rubiah nodded to confirm. 'I don't think she's made up her mind yet what to do.'

'Do you think he'd divorce Khatijah?' Maryam asked Noriah. 'I mean, really...'

'He hasn't got the nerve,' Noriah said sadly. 'Though he would if he had any sense. Anyway, you know they adopted a child? And him with seven already he doesn't do a thing for. That's Khatijah.

She always wanted a family.'

'She never had any herself?'

Noriah shook her head. 'I don't think she ever stayed married long enough, if you know what I mean. Wandered around.' Noriah said this with disapproval, as befitted a woman who had paid attention to her future and ensured she was provided for. Not for her to be *seperti apong di permain gelombang* – like driftwood, a sport of the waves, a woman of no importance. That Khatijah had allowed herself to become this was incomprehensible, in fact, it was diametrically opposed to the world view of Kelantanese womanhood and the *Mak Cik* code: hard work, control over finances, running the household and subservience to no one. Maryam and Rubiah could hardly have agreed more emphatically.

Noriah pulled out a plastic bag with home-rolled cigarettes from the waist of her sarong, and offered them around. A young woman padded softly onto the porch and refilled coffee, adding more cakes to the plate. She smiled shyly and withdrew, leaving the three women with some privacy. They lit up and leaned back against whatever was at hand: Noriah against a wall, Maryam and Rubiah each with their own house post.

'Did Yusuf have any other businesses where someone might have been angry at him?' Rubiah asked after a deep and satisfying drag on her cigarette. How pleasant – well, relatively, to be able to speak to one's own people in one's own *kampong*, she reflected, rather than travelling all over the state looking for suspects. Given her preference, Rubiah would have had all suspects brought to her rather than have to search them out in either the heat and dust of the dry season, or the unremitting damp of the monsoon. She did not care for travel.

'Not really,' Noriah replied easily. 'Well, he liked *merbok* and singing competitions,' she smiled at Maryam, the two having met each other at various local contests, 'but that isn't a business.'

'A hobby, then,' Maryam smiled back. 'Did he also go to Ah Pak's to talk birds?'

'Endlessly!' Noriah laughed.

'Where did he buy his birds?' Maryam leaned forward, interested not only for the investigation, but for general bird information that perhaps could be of use to Mamat.

Noriah sighed. 'I don't really know everywhere he went for them. He was in Thailand a lot to buy … supplies. Maybe there? Ah Pak might know: he might have bought from him directly. I didn't really go with him to look for them.'

Maryam nodded. It was a man's thing, that was true.

'Well,' Rubiah said, preparatory to leaving, 'Thank you. You've been so much help to us.'

'I want you to find whoever did this to Yusuf. He wasn't perfect, I know that, but he didn't deserve this.' Her eyes suddenly filled with tears for the first time since his death, surprising her with the welling up of emotion she had not yet had. She swallowed hard, and avoided their eyes. 'I will help however I can.'

Maryam and Rubiah smiled sympathetically and added extra pats on the shoulder as they took their leave.

# Chapter VII

Clouds were gathering ominously over Kelantan. The rains hadn't yet begun, but the dry season was clearly drawing to an imminent close. This was always a time of year Maryam found full of anticipation: the winds picked up, it was cooler and wetter as a prelude to the monsoon She was sick of the heat, but not yet sick of the humidity brought by the rain, the interminably damp laundry and mold growing on everything that didn't actively move. Right now, the rains and possible – probable? – floods looked like a party.

Osman sent Rahman to drive them to their interviews: he did not want to risk their being caught in a sudden rain. At any rate, Maryam was used to having a car and Rahman at her disposal while detecting. Rahman had been badly hurt while heroically chasing down a suspect (who was indeed the murderer) through the Kota Bharu market, and for a while, his recovery was despaired of. A head injury left him forgetful and slow-talking, but this had been improving, and he was bouncing back to normal. His good nature, remarkable under the circumstances, carried him through his injuries and now through his nearly complete recovery. Such was his progress, his mother began looking for a wife for him, deciding he would be capable of surviving without her care.

Ruslan's small house was in the city of Kota Bharu, on Jalan Tengku Cik, down a small alley behind a Chinese coffee shop selling dumpling soup during the day. It was invisible from the street unless you knew where to look for the alley, and Maryam, Rubiah and Rahman spent several minutes walking back and forth until the coffee shop owner noticed them and guided them with amusement back to the house. Here, only yards away from a busy paved street, the *kampong* reasserted itself, and chickens roamed the swept dirt yards.

Munira looked terrified to see them. She looked past Maryam and Rubiah to the genial Rahman, and lost all colour in her face: Maryam feared she would swoon right there in the doorway. Rubiah stepped forward to distract Munira, forcing her to look directly at her and away from the policeman who mesmerized her.

'*Kakak,*' she began loudly, 'How are you? *Kakak* Maryam and I are here helping the police investigate *Che* Yusuf's unfortunate ...' She was reluctant to say 'death' to someone so obviously near to fainting already. 'May we come in?'

The whites of Munira's eyes could be seen below the brown iris, giving her a wildly uncontrolled look, which quite spooked Maryam. She smiled thinly and looked for a place to sit a bit removed from her hostess, who might lose her sanity altogether. Rahman, as always, seemed serenely unaffected, and sat quietly in the corner with his small notebook, a pleasant and neutral expression on his face.

Munira had said nothing: neither words of welcome or offering or hospitality, but stood in front of them, her eyes rolling and hands clutching at each other, panting for breath. 'Are you alright, *Kakak*?' Rubiah asked kindly, but received no answer.

Maryam stood up and, placing her hands on Munira's shoulders, led her to a seat on the small and ragged sofa and pushed her down onto it. Maryam and Rubiah sat on either side of her, radiating concern. Rubiah reached over and stroked her arm, believing this kind of firm, steady touch often relieved stress, and calmed people almost immediately. It brought down the rate of Munira's breathing, which was at least a start.

'Are you alright? She repeated.

'Are you here about my husband?' Munira whispered, making motions with her hands together as though washing them, unable to stop or even slow them down.

'What about him?' Rubiah asked gently.

'You've … you've found him?'

'Where did he go?'

'I don't know,' she wailed. 'He hasn't been home for two days. I don't know where he is, or even if he's alive.'

'I think you'd better start from the beginning, *Kakak*,' Maryam advised her, separating Munira's grasping hands and placing them at her sides. She offered her one of her cigarettes, hoping this activity would stop the other, and it appeared to work. Munira held the cigarette in both hands as though she might drink it, and then looked sharply around her.

'Who are you?' she asked.

'I am Rubiah and this is Maryam,' she explained, and waved her hand toward Rahman. 'He is from the Kota Bharu Police, whom we are helping. We're looking into *Che* Yusuf's passing.'

'Why?'

'Well, someone killed him, *Kakak*, and we want to help bring this person to justice.'

Munira's hands began to tremble. 'He was not a good man.'

'Tell me,' Maryam urged.

'I shouldn't really. I mean, it could mean trouble for us, for my husband. He's had some bad luck, you know, it's been very difficult for him.'

Maryam and Rubiah arranged their expressions to show concern and sympathy, erasing any trace of either disapproval or disbelief.

'Ruslan gambles a bit,' she began, resisting the urge to twist her hands once more. 'I mean, it isn't anything serious.' She looked at them to see if they believed her. They did not, but made no comment nor did their faces twitch. 'And he's had a run of bad luck, oh yes! Terrible. I thought perhaps someone had placed a *jampi* on him to deprive him of his luck. I still don't know ...' Her voice petered out.

'Had he been lucky before?'

She seemed puzzled. 'Well, you know ... sometimes you are, sometimes not. But this seemed different because it went on for so long, and ...' she paused here for effect. 'He lost *a lot* of money. A lot.'

'Where did he get a lot of money to lose?' Maryam asked,

fearing she already knew the answer.

'*Che* Yusuf lent it to him.' Maryam had been correct. 'I mean, at the house, he lent it to him while he was playing so he could keep going. And then, when he was finished, he'd lost all of that and now owed Yusuf all this money, which we don't have.'

A quick perusal of the room confirmed that. 'Did *Che* Yusuf come here to talk about it?'

She nodded, and commenced twisting her hands again. Maryam stifled the urge to slap them apart and make her sit on them to keep them still.

'He came here. Just once, last week, I think. He just spoke to us, very polite, but I knew. Oh yes, I knew what would happen next. I've known Yusuf for a while, and I've heard stories. He gets paid back, one way or another.

'I knew it as soon as I saw him walk up to the house. "Munira," I said to myself, "you're in trouble now."' She nodded, and looked philosophical. 'Ruslan always tries to see things in a good light, and he thinks everything will work out, but I knew, no matter how friendly Yusuf looked, it was bad.'

'When did Ruslan leave?' Maryam asked gently.

She thought for a moment. 'The next day he went out to talk to people. About money, you see.'

'Who?' Rubiah pressed her.

'I don't know,' she said sadly. 'I don't know anyone who could lend us that kind of money. Maybe go to a money lender? But we'd never get out from under something like that. We'd be ruined either way: *ludah mati pak, telan mati mak* – spit it out and your father dies, swallow it and your mother dies. We're doomed, and now he's gone. I don't know what will become of us.' She brightened momentarily. 'Since *Che* Yusuf is gone now, do you think *Cik* Noriah will forgive the debt? It's possible, right?'

Maryam thought it most unlikely that Noriah would begin her tenure as the sole owner of a gambling den with a general amnesty, but didn't want to dash Munira's hopes immediately. Maybe she would forgive just this one, as the circumstances were so dire. But then, didn't every one of the gamblers have dire circumstances surrounding their debt? Children to be fed, spouses to be cared for, homes they could not afford to lose. Each one had a story, Maryam was sure, and even so, they gambled away the rent money, or the food money, or – in Ruslan's case – absolutely everything. It was depressing to consider. She shrugged and smiled sadly, as if to indicate she had no insight into what Noriah might do.

'Where did you think he had gone?'

Munira shifted her eyes, minimally yet unmistakably, and Maryam and Rubiah both knew at that moment she was lying about something, or omitting something at least. 'I didn't know,' she maintained.

'You are very close to your husband, aren't you? It's a real marriage, where you share everything, isn't it?' Rubiah smiled, indicating her admiration for that kind of relationship.

Munira nodded, now looking nervous again.

'So you'd know,' Rubiah continued gently, 'where he was going, wouldn't you? He wasn't the sort of husband to just leave and not tell you where he was going?'

Munira looked from one to the other, licking her lips and tugging at her sarong. 'I don't know,' she repeated faintly.

With sudden inspiration, Maryam asked, 'Did he leave the next morning, or did he go out after *Che* Yusuf left?'

Munira burst into tears, sobbing and pulling at her hair. Malay society did not encourage operatic displays of emotion, and her guests were shocked into inaction when confronted by it. Maryam gingerly put her arm around Munira's shoulder while she bent double at the waist and howled. She looked beseechingly toward Rahman, who approached Munira as he would an angry snake and, with extreme caution, picked her up and deposited her back onto the sofa. Rubiah disappeared into the kitchen to make coffee or anything else she could locate. She thought this might go on for awhile.

'There, there,' Maryam cooed, hoping her distaste didn't show, though Munira was too far gone to notice if it had. 'Now,' she offered a package of tissues from her purse, 'tell me all about it. That's the only way you're going to feel better.'

Rahman retreated back to the corner, willing Maryam and Rubiah to take care of it. After all, they were the *Mak Ciks*, and their all-around competence should surely extend to this. It took Maryam several long minutes to calm Munira down to the point where she could speak coherently, if not completely truthfully. Rubiah acted as hostess, pouring out coffee for everyone and passing out cigarettes. Maryam shook her head at Munira, not allowing her to smoke until it was clear she wouldn't choke.

'Now,' Maryam ordered, patting Munira on her damp knee, 'tell us what happened. What *really* happened.'

# Chapter VIII

Munira gave a few exploratory sniffs, as if to test her ability to breathe. She then straightened herself, squared her shoulders, and looked bravely at Maryam.

'Yusuf came here to ask for his money. You don't know how he does it, but I've heard about it, so I knew what to expect. This was his first visit, so no one was hurt.' Maryam and Rubiah exchanged looks.

'Oh yes,' Munira assured them, 'I know how this goes. People talk. First he comes to talk to you, nice and friendly. You're going to work out a schedule and pay him back. But, there's a problem. Where are you going to get the money for that? Who will lend it to you? No one. Just Yusuf, and the interest is high and you can never get out. Soon, he'll take any land you own or your house. *Macam pacat melompat,* like a jumping leech. Then you're nothing anymore.'

Maryam and Rubiah exchanged a look, surprised at how much one could miss about what went on below the surface of everyday life.

'So we knew, this was the start of our disaster.'

'Wasn't it gambling that was the start of your disaster?' asked Rubiah blandly. 'I mean, once you'd lost all that money you knew this was coming next.' She pursed her lips, unwilling to allow Munira to paint herself as the innocent victim.

Munira gave her a dirty look and ignored her. 'When he came, we knew. *Tinggal kelopak salak:* only the *salak* (snakefruit) wrapper is left. We'd be destitute. We were doomed. We'd lose everything and it was all over for us.' She sighed, and wiped away more tears.

'Well, when he left, what could we do? We looked at each other, Ruslan and I, and I tell you, *Kakak*, all I wanted to do was die. What future was there for us? No money, no home, no land, everywhere people would look at us and whisper. I couldn't face it.'

She buried her face once again in her hands and sobbed. Maryam again patted her shoulder absently, growing tired of this endless sobbing. How did gambling always end? Never with the gambler becoming rich, that was certain.

'Ruslan said he would go to talk to his older brother: maybe he would help him. I didn't care if he did, but I didn't think it would help, either. He left soon after Yusuf did, and he came back about two hours later. Just as I thought, his brother didn't want to do anything to help: he only wanted to lecture him about how it was his own fault.' Munira made a face. 'It's no help at all.'

'Where does his brother live?' Rubiah asked.

'In Kampong Dusun Muda, Jalan Bayam,' she indicated the direction with her head. 'Not too far.'

'How did he look when he got back?'

Munira was no longer sniffling and seemed to have become more argumentative. 'How should he have looked? The same way he left.'

'I mean, was he muddy or anything?'

She snorted. 'There's no mud yet,' she reminded them. 'Not in the middle of Kota Bharu.' She was quiet for a moment. 'I know, you're asking me if he killed Yusuf.' She nodded. 'I know it. But I don't think he did … I think whoever killed Yusuf killed Ruslan.' She began crying again. 'I think he's dead. Why else would he stay away?'

'Have you spoken to his brother?' Maryam interrupted.

Munira shook her head. 'I haven't spoken to anyone. I don't want to see anyone.'

'Has anyone come to see you about the money you owned Yusuf?' Rubiah was curious as to whether Noriah had gotten right to work.

Munira shook her head. 'Not yet. *Cik* Noriah hasn't really started the business up again.' She sighed. 'It won't take long, though.'

'What's the brother's name?' Maryam asked briskly, anxious to be away from Munira's damp self-pity. As often happened when she was presented with characters weaker than her own, she longed to slap them into shape, though she knew it would be socially unacceptable. It was time for her to leave, before she surrendered to the urge.

'Yunus. Just ask when you get to Dusun Muda, everyone will

know who he is.'

Maryam nodded, and forced herself to smile and pat Munira's shoulder. 'I'm sure Ruslan will be back, who knows where he's gone to? Maybe up to Thailand to win back the money.' If that were the case, then he'd certainly deserve whatever happened to him there, she reflected. It would be even more monumentally stupid than what he had done so far, and that was saying something.'

Munira said nothing, staring glumly at the floor. 'I don't know,' she said finally, summing up the full account of how she felt about her life at the moment.'

# Chapter IX

Yunus' house was a brisk walk through Kota Bharu, past the market (which Maryam gazed at longingly, wishing she was presiding over her own stall as she was meant to do), past the roundabout that led to the hospital, past the soccer stadium, and finally past the Sikh temple on Jalan Bayam to one of the largest urban *kampong*, Dusun Muda. Two steps off the street and it was indistinguishable from any rural village, with packed dirt roads, roaming chickens and unconcerned goats, and a profusion of fruit trees and coconut palms. It was much like Kampong Penambang, and Maryam liked it far more than she had Jalan Tengku Cik, with its constant traffic, noise and the smell of diesel fuel. This village was at least out of the true centre of the city and much quieter.

Munira was correct: the first person they stopped directed them to *Che* Yunus' house, which was one of the larger homes they saw, with a wide-roofed verandah and cement stairs. It looked neat and prosperous, and it was hard to imagine the owner's brother was a penniless gambler with absolutely no prospects, both a murder suspect and possibly a victim, with a sobbing (and, if Maryam could be completely honest, most irritating) wife.

As they approached the house, the woman putting the final touches on a perfectly swept yard looked up curiously. 'Good afternoon,' she said politely, the question of what they were doing there clearly in her eyes. Rubiah introduced them, but the woman seemed more unsure. 'I know who you are,' she finally said. 'I've heard of you. But ... why are you here?'

'Your brother-in-law, Ruslan ...'

'Him? Oh you mean ... Yusuf. Oh. I see.' With a resigned shrug, she motioned for them to go up to the verandah, and called inside to have their refreshments delivered. After they arrived, they were followed by her husband, an older man: where Ruslan was thin and bent, he was hale and well set-up and carried himself confidently. He had full, thick silver hair and a round face, which was still imposing and would have been very handsome indeed in his youth. He smiled all around, and then sat down on the porch, squinting into the sunlight, listening idly as his wife fielded all questions.

Rubiah began. 'How long has Ruslan been gambling?'

Nuraini, Yunus' wife, shot her husband a hooded glance before continuing, while he maintained a Buddha-like serenity. 'He's always been wild, even as a teenager,' she told them earnestly. 'It was a big family, and he was one of the younger ones, so more *manja*, spoiled than the older kids. My husband is the eldest. So I would have to say Ruslan's been more or less in trouble all the time since he was fifteen or so. He never grew up.'

She looked disapproving, as did they all. Who had time for

that kind of nonsense when you were trying to earn a living and raise a family? 'I guess it's lucky he and Munira didn't have any children; they'd never be able to take care of them.'

She paused for a moment, thinking. 'You know, now she's as bad as he is, but that wasn't how it used to be. She was a nice girl, and he ruined her. His parents should never have arranged a marriage for him, and they would have avoided dragging some poor girl into his mess.' She looked at her husband, who nodded blandly but said nothing.

'He came here last week. I gather Yusuf had paid a call on him and he realized he was actually being asked to pay back what he lost, and quickly too. He was panicked. Right, Nus?'

Finally, Yunus spoke. Maryam leaned forward to hear him. 'Panicked, yes, that's the right word. He had no way of getting any money: not the kind of money he owed.'

'How much was that?' Rubiah asked.

Yunus looked uncomfortable. 'A lot,' he answered slowly. Rubiah looked enquiringly at him, awaiting a more solid answer. 'Over 5,000 ringgit,' Yunus muttered.

Maryam was aghast. How could anyone come up with that kind of money, and for what? Nothing. Gambling. No wonder Munira said they were ruined. Maryam had wondered whether she was being dramatic, but now she thought she was downplaying it. It was an enormous amount of money.

'Alamak!' she blurted. Yunus nodded.

'Amazing, isn't it, that Yusuf would let him run it up that high? I guess he thought he'd take his land, but he can't. You

68

see, I had it signed over to me after the last time I bailed him out, so he had nothing in his name anymore. Yusuf was bound to be unhappy when he realized it.' Yunus, on the other hand, looked quite satisfied at the thought. 'Rus just couldn't be trusted,' he said sadly.

'What happened last week?'

Yunus shook his head. 'I can't do it anymore. I told him that. It's not as if it's an emergency, now it's just what he does all the time. And the sums! This is a lot of money! I told him to go, I couldn't help him.'

'Was he angry?'

Yunus considered this. 'Maybe a little. But not so much angry as … desperate. He knew why I said no, I think he understood it. But he wasn't thinking clearly, he just wanted a way out, and I couldn't give it to him. He asked me what he would do now.' Yunus looked sad again. 'I didn't know. I couldn't tell him anything. And then he left.'

'And you haven't seen him since?'

Yunus shook his head again. 'Munira says he's gone?'

Maryam nodded. 'Since the morning after he spoke to you.'

'That's a long time.'

'Yes, it is,' she agreed.

He sighed. 'I hope he's alright. But I fear he isn't.'


Suleiman and Khatijah had completed their disgrace, living in one of the most ramshackle homes either Maryam or Rubiah had ever seen. The house itself looked slovenly, listing slightly to the side as if too lazy to actually stand up straight. It was on the other side of Kota Bharu, towards Pengkalan Cepa, behind some shop houses. It slouched alone, as an afterthought, not part of a *kampong*. Maryam thought it an apt symbol of Suleiman's current status: outside the web of Malay society, alone, untethered, disreputable. She purposely tried to smooth her face of all expression, so her disapproval would not show and her quarry would not be reluctant to speak with her.

Khatijah came to the door before Maryam and Rubiah could ascend to the house, and greeted them effusively. Maryam surmised they received very few visitors.

'Come in, come in,' she urged them with a broad smile, 'get out of the sun. It's too hot, isn't it? Come, *Mak Cik*, have something to drink and be comfortable.'

She held out a hand to help them up the last rung of the ladder to the tiny porch, and into the living room, which was small and airless. They smiled and sat on the floor, leaning against the wall nearest the door, hoping for a breath of air. Khatijah bustled into the kitchen and began making tea.

'How nice of you to stop by! Of course, I've heard of you. You're the famous *Mak Cik* detectives,' Rubiah winced to hear it. 'So clever! I admire you, being so brave and smart,' she chattered on.

Maryam and Rubiah looked around the bare room, with only two *tikar*, sleeping mats, rolled up in a corner. Other than that, the room was bare, with little sign of habitation. Maryam looked for traces of Suleiman's presence, or that of the child she heard they'd adopted, but the room remained empty. Khatijah kept up a stream of talk they barely listened to, before reappearing from the kitchen carrying three teacups and four home-rolled cigarettes on a plate.

'*Jangan susah susah,* don't trouble yourself,' Maryam admonished her as she placed the tray on the floor in front of them. 'No trouble at all,' Khatijah said happily and Maryam, who had come in already disliking her, felt herself melt somewhat towards her. After all, she was a cheerful and enthusiastic hostess, and that meant something.

'Where is Suleiman?' Maryam asked with an air of confusion. 'Isn't he here? I understand you're married now.'

Khatijah made a face, and some of her happiness seemed to evaporate. 'Well … it was very short-lived,' she admitted, subdued. 'He registered one *talak* yesterday and went back to his … home.' She smiled again, regaining her spirits. 'It wasn't very long we were married. Maybe a mistake, you know.'

She put her hand on Maryam's arm. 'He has seven kids already, you know. Too many to leave, I think. Maybe we both got carried away when we got married, but then we began to think about it, really think about it, and it couldn't really work.'

She didn't seem all that upset by it, and her explanation raised her significantly in Maryam's estimation. She found herself actually liking Khatijah, which surprised her. And even more, the woman no longer looked quite as dark, or as small, as Maryam had formerly considered her.

'Did I hear correctly, you adopted a child?'

Khatijah smiled, a smile of pure delight. 'A daughter, yes. She's at my mother's now.' She reached into the folds of her sarong, unrolling it slightly, and removed a small photograph of a Chinese girl of about a year-and-a-half. A pretty girl, with a big smile and thick, straight hair. 'Siti Hawa,' she announced grandly. She sat back and radiated pride.

'So nice,' both Maryam and Rubiah cooed, admiring the photo, pointing out her fine features. 'So cute!'

'She's wonderful,' the proud mother said shyly, blushing a little, clearly in love with the child. 'People say she's very smart. I'm moving back to my mother's house at the end of this month,' she confided. 'I need her help taking care of the baby, and what's the point of just us living out here in the middle of nowhere? My mother's in Kampong Tikat,' she named a village a bit farther out of the city than Kampong Penambang. 'I'm happy to move back there. Siti Hawa will have friends – you know, her family. Much better than here. This place is terrible,' she opined, looking around the bare room 'Don't you think so?'

They returned her honesty. 'I was surprised when I saw it,' Maryam admitted. 'So isolated.'

Khatijah nodded. 'I thought so too when I saw it. Suleiman found it. He's not much of a character, if you know what I mean. *Kerbau cucuk hidung,* a buffalo with a ring through his nose. He just wants to be led around.

'Well,' she sighed, 'I guess I just wanted to get married, you know, have a father for my daughter. He was the wrong one, and besides, he's got plenty of children already to be a father to, if he wants to. I don't think he's very interested, and I'll tell you,' she leaned forward, 'I can't say I have much respect for him when he doesn't take care of them.'

She thought for a moment. 'That sounds strange coming from me, doesn't it, *Mak Cik*? Since I married him. I mean, knowing he was such a terrible father to his own kids. But it was a mistake, and now it's corrected.' She looked at them seriously, and then her expression changed to a happier, more light-hearted one. 'More tea?'

Maryam smiled and accepted. She cleared her throat, as introduction to topics she was now reluctant to broach, but was compelled to, nevertheless.

'What was it? That is, was anything, you know ...' she paused, knowing she was getting nowhere with this. It was time to get on with it. She took a deep breath. 'Was anything going on with *Cik* Yusuf?' she asked Khatijah. 'I understand that when you married, at the celebration, he was watching you very closely. Why?'

Khatijah did not seem offended. She considered her answer. 'Nothing between us, not like it sounds when you say it, *Mak Cik*. Never!' she said vehemently. 'You know, *Cik* Noriah doesn't like me. That's OK, I don't like her either, but I'm not angry at her, do you know what I mean?

'*Cik* Yusuf, though,' she paused. 'He was not a good man. I know he's died and we should be careful what we say about him, but do you know what he wanted? He wanted me to work as a prostitute! Yes, in the parlour. He said people wanted to do that when they gambled; it was part of the thrill, he said.

'I don't know if *Cik* Noriah knew about it,' she said, anticipating Maryam's next question. 'I didn't ask her about it. But I told him no. Maybe that's another reason why I married Suleiman,' she mused, 'to make sure he wouldn't ask me again, though knowing him, he probably would have anyway.'

Her anger flashed suddenly, and just as suddenly disappeared. 'That's probably why he was watching me like that at the celebration. He was angry I said no, and even angrier that I got married so quickly. That sealed my 'no'.

'You know what he told me then? If I didn't want to do it, he could find another girl. "Never mind," he said. "You're not the only girl around." Like this was a chance for something great. Can you imagine?' She shook her head angrily.

'As though Siti Hawa's mother would be a prostitute. How would that be for her? As if I would do that to her. I'm her mother now,' she said, her cheeks getting redder, 'I can't do things like that. Not,' she amended, 'that I ever would.'

'Did Suleiman know?'

She nodded, avoiding Maryam's eyes. 'I told him. He didn't say anything, really. He said he was surprised, but he didn't seem angry. That surprised me. If it were my wife, I'd be furious.'

'Did he say anything to Yusuf?'

'I doubt it,' she said with asperity. 'I don't think he had the nerve! He'd just look sheepish in front of Yusuf. Probably owed him money.'

'What do you know about Zainuddin?'

'The gambler, Zainuddin?' She seemed mystified.

Maryam nodded. 'I hear he owed Yusuf a lot of money.'

'He did,' Khatijah confirmed. 'He always lost. Well, in the end, they all do, don't they?'

'What's he like?'

'He has a temper. Kind of the opposite of Suleiman, in a way. Though they both gambled, which is a lot. But Suleiman wanted to be led around, like I said. Zainuddin wanted to lead, even though he was ... stupid.'

'Really?'

She raised her eyebrows and made a face which said, 'Of course!'

'He never thought at all. Just went from happy to angry in a few seconds. But he's big and strong, so angry and not smart is a dangerous combination for him.'

'Had he ever fought with Yusuf?'

'Of course! Whenever Yusuf tried to collect some of the money he owed. Yusuf was also big and strong, so neither of them was likely to give in. Yusuf, for all I really didn't like him, was smart. He'd never let Zainuddin get away without paying.'

'Had it happened before?'

'A few years ago. And believe me, Din paid up. He wouldn't dare cross Yusuf like that.'

'Do you think he could have ... hurt him?'

'You mean, killed him? I don't know. He might try. Like I said, Din was stupid, and if he got mad, he'd just do whatever came into his head.'

'Does he owe money right now?'

She nodded. 'Yusuf was just talking to him about it a little while ago. I don't think it went very well, though usually, after the first time Yusuf's collected, they pay up much faster the second time. Yusuf can – could be, I mean – tough.'

Maryam rose to thank her hostess with newfound warmth. 'Stop by sometime in Kampong Tikat,' Khatijah urged them both. 'Come and meet my daughter! I'm thinking of opening a little coffee stand on the main road. We'll see ...' She laughed happily, and Maryam liked her even more.

# Chapter X

Zainuddin lived with his long-suffering wife and two nearly grown children near the match factory in Kota Bharu, in an insalubrious collection of houses on the bank of the river. Mud was a constant here; it never seemed to dry, and the houses were mired in it. Maryam and Rubiah held their sarongs up out of the dirt and kept to the single plywood board road, which rocked every time they put a foot on it. Maryam feared for her equilibrium and silently cursed the narrow tightrope she was forced to walk. Rubiah did not bother with silence, but grumbled audibly and occasionally turned to grasp Rahman's arm to keep herself erect. It was but a short walk from the main, paved road, but already the two were sweating profusely with the effort of balancing.

Zainuddin's wife stood in the doorway, watching them expressionlessly. When they arrived at her door, she gestured for them to come up the ladder without saying a word, and when they had entered the living room, she'd already disappeared, leaving her husband to entertain their guests. He'd recently woken up, though it was well into late morning, and he sat before them in a spavined chair scratching himself. Maryam detested him on sight.

He looked both sleepy and sulky, with heavy cheekbones and thick lips. He was as described, big and broad, and didn't look too bright. His eyes were only half opened, his nose was wide and his hair was standing on end. As Maryam summed him up: *All in all, a hot mess.* He gave them a perfunctory smile and evinced no curiosity regarding them or why they were there.

He wandered over to a small cabinet and rummaged through it to extract a crumpled cigarette pack, which he examined with tremendous interest and care, to find two cigarettes still in it. He grinned apologetically at the women, took one for himself and offered his last to Rahman in an unforgiveable breach of courtesy. Maryam and Rubiah exchanged a look, and then each brought out her own cigarettes. If he had no manners, at least they could make themselves comfortable!

He yawned. 'What are you doing here?' he asked at last, finally registering that he didn't know them, and they must have some errand in mind. Rahman answered immediately, as he rarely did, hoping as a policeman to get his attention.

'We're here to investigate *Che* Yusuf's murder,' he began crisply, 'and we understand you're one of his regulars.'

Rahman looked at him boldly, challenging him to wake up and start thinking, but Din merely scratched with more effort. He took a long drag on his cigarette, and watched his wife enter with coffee and a small plate of cookies. She served, wordless, and retreated to the kitchen while Din vaguely waved his hands over the cups, picked one up and began slurping.

Rubiah closed her eyes to avoid the spectacle of a Malay man acting like a complete boor. *Berapa tingginya terbang bagau, akhirnya hinggap dibelakang kerbau juga:* no matter how high the *padi* bird flies, it ends up on a water buffalo's back. Din could not be schooled and taught courtesy, and would always revert to the ill-mannered lout he now appeared to be. She sighed with resignation and thanked heaven she was not related to him.

Maryam began asking questions, determined to get out of this house, and across that infernal mud, as quickly as possible. 'Did you owe Yusuf money?' she asked, dispensing with any gracious preliminaries she judged would go unnoticed by their host. Why waste time? 'I heard you had rather large debts.'

Din continued to look unconcerned, but Maryam thought she detected a flash in his eye indicating some brain activity. He shrugged. 'Not too bad.'

'Didn't Yusuf come to talk to you? You were one of his largest debtors.'

'Me?' he asked innocently. 'I don't think so.'

'Zainuddin,' Maryam began in her sternest tones, 'We know it happened, and we've seen the records. If you want to pretend no one knows anything, we'll see you at the police station and you can talk there.' She narrowed her eyes so he'd know she meant business. 'Now pay attention.'

Din looked surprised that his obfuscation didn't work. Khatijah was right: stupid.

'Now,' Rubiah chimed in, 'How much did you owe Yusuf this time?' Din looked at her and she nodded. 'Oh yes, we know it wasn't the first time you've gotten into trouble. How much?'

He looked back and forth between them with his jaw slack. Rubiah wanted nothing more than to send him to his room with a hard smack across the ear and tell him to get dressed, comb his hair, and come back with a change of attitude. Apparently, this had not been done often enough when he was a boy and still might have learned something from it.

He mumbled something they could not catch. Rahman demanded clarification and, reluctantly and sulkily, he said, 'Around 3,000 Ringgit.'

Maryam was once more amazed at the debts run up gambling. 'How will you pay it?' she blurted out before thinking.

Din began to bluster. 'I have ways, you know. I have plans. I have some rice land near Pantai Sabak, and I'm thinking maybe I can rent it out to someone – '

Maryam cut him off. 'You mean Yusuf would have taken your rice land for himself? And then you'll lose it completely! What will you leave your children?'

'Why do you care?'

'I don't,' Maryam answered honestly. 'But you should, as their father.'

'It's none of your business,' Din told her with perfect accuracy. 'I'll do –'

Rubiah interrupted, anxious to return to the matter at hand. 'What did you talk to Yusuf about then? How did he want to collect the debt?'

'Well, you know, this and that.'

'Din!' Rubiah admonished him. 'Stop it.' She could no longer control herself. 'Comb your hair, sit down and start talking like an adult. I never saw anything like this, greeting visitors, police visitors, by scratching yourself and acting like you're in the middle of taking a bath. Have you no manners! *Kurang ajar!* Insufficiently taught. It's a disgrace.'

She looked around at Maryam and Rahman to back her up. Rahman seemed amused, Maryam delighted. 'You heard her,' she ordered Din. 'Act like an adult.'

Din seemed stupefied by the dressing-down he'd received. He smoothened his hair with both hands and pulled his undershirt down, patting the front. He then stared at Rubiah with empty, though not hostile, eyes.

It was a perfunctory, badly done job, which Rubiah would never have accepted from her own children, or those of her friends and relatives, but it was probably the best she'd get from Zainuddin. She snorted in derision and launched back into her interrogation.

'Yusuf was going to take your land, wasn't he?' Din nodded as though hypnotized, like a mouse watching a snake. 'Had he taken other land before, the last time you were in trouble?'

Din squirmed slightly and had the grace to look embarrassed. 'My *kakak* gave me some of her land to pay it off.'

'And you were supposed to pay it back?' He nodded again. 'And you never will,' she concluded with irritation. 'You just took her land and squandered it.' Maryam laid a calming hand on her arm, warning her it might not do to berate witnesses into submission, but Din had clearly set her off. 'Now that Yusuf is dead, do you think that means your debt won't need to be paid?'

At this, Din seemed to come alive. 'I think it's all over. After all, I owed it to Yusuf, and he's dead, so now I don't owe anything to anyone.'

Maryam was happy to disabuse him of his fantasy. 'Not true, I'm afraid. *Cik* Noriah will take it over, and she'll expect payment from you, don't you worry. Debts like that don't just disappear.'

He looked stricken. He'd already counted on the debt's cancellation. 'Where were you last week when Yusuf died?'

He didn't answer, but began to look frightened. 'Well?' Rahman demanded. 'Where were you?'

'I don't remember. I don't know. What day was it?'

'Tuesday.'

'I was … away. In Thailand.'

'Where?'

'Tak Bai. I was playing there. There's a place.'

'Do you owe money there, too?'

He didn't answer, clearly unable to process anymore. Rubiah, just as clearly, lost all patience with the process and stood up abruptly. 'Thank you,' she said shortly, and headed for the ladder and the plank path. Bemused, Maryam and Rahman followed, picking their way slowly, painstakingly, across the mud to the blessed safety of the road.

# Chapter XI

Mamat, who was usually interested in Maryam's investigation and happy to help if he could, now had bigger fish to fry: the competition he'd been training for was only days away. He no longer made the pretense of concern for anything other than his birds, who he obsessively groomed, fed and fretted over.

Much of his day now was spent at Ah Pak's store. Though in many other contests they might be competitors, Ah Pak was sitting out this particular one and was therefore acting in the capacity of Mamat's coach and mentor. They discussed the birds' food endlessly, and practiced running them in their cages up a pole planted in front of the store for just such a purpose. The men stood at the bottom of the pole, watching their star bird, Borek, hop around in his cage and then begin to sing. Mamat smiled delightedly, and Ah Pak watched him like a proud father.

'He'll do very well,' he informed a rapt Mamat. 'Look at him: so confident, so natural. He has no fear at all,' he said approvingly. 'That's what a champion can do.'

He nodded, smiling. He believed his regimen of specific foods, seeds and oils had developed Borek's personality into the great performer they now hoped he was. Ah Pak enjoyed coaching and managing, teaching the ropes to someone not quite as experienced as he was himself, and Mamat had been a friend and a fellow aficionado for many years.

'Mamat,' he began hesitantly, in a tone altogether unrelated to the full-throated acclaim he'd just given to Borek, 'there's something …'

'What?' Mamat remained jubilant, his eye on his bird.

'No, it's not about the bird. It's something else.'

His tone caused Mamat to tear himself away from the cage at the top of the pole and direct his attention to Ah Pak. 'What's the matter?'

Ah Pak cleared his throat, clearly unhappy with raising the issue. 'I understand … that is, I hear that your wife is investigating Yusuf's death. You know, the one who owned the gambling place in his parents' old house.'

'My wife is quite a detective,' Mamat agreed, still cheerful. 'She's working on it, but she'll be there at the competition to cheer for Borek. She wouldn't miss it, you know. She loves the birds also.'

'Good. But that isn't what I wanted to talk to you about. You see,' he took a deep breath, 'I've had problems with Yusuf before. For myself and for Kit Siang. He's a wild boy, but a good one. He was gambling a little, you know,' Ah Pak now looked supremely uncomfortable, but plowed ahead with determination nevertheless.

'I spoke to Yusuf about letting the boy run up large debts. He's just a kid, I told him, throw him out when he starts losing serious money. Don't encourage him to keep going and then come to me to pay up.' Mamat listened quietly, hearing the hurt in his friend's voice. 'He knew I'd pay. I'd never let him hurt Kit Siang. That's what he depended on, you see, that whenever he came to me with the debt, no matter how much I'd complain, I wouldn't tell him to collect from my son. He knew that, and he kept coming back to me.

'I had to get Kit Siang away from all this. He's got to grow up. I don't say he's not to blame here; after all, Yusuf didn't drag him in to gamble, and it was Kit Siang who kept going back. I know that. But Yusuf was like a spider, waiting for him to be weak, and then jumping on him. And me, too.'

Ah Pak looked morose, as all joy over the bird evaporated. 'I sent him to my sister's in Gua Musang. That should be far enough away for him to stay out of trouble. And she's looking for a wife for him: all my sisters are down there and they're all looking.' He began to cheer up. 'Believe me, if all my sisters are looking for a wife, they'll find one! And when he's married, you know, he'll settle down. He wants to, it isn't that. He hated what happened with Yusuf, and he blamed himself, I didn't have to say a word to him.'

'How many times did Yusuf come to you?' Mamat asked gently.

'Three times he came to see me. He has a way about him, it's scary but not obvious. He doesn't say anything directly to you, but you know what he means and what will happen if you don't pay. Kit Siang's mother would never forgive me if I let anything happen. I'd never forgive myself, either. But I tell you as a friend, I'm not sorry Yusuf's dead. He deserved it.'

'Why are you telling me this?'

Ah Pak seemed to wrestle with the words to explain himself. 'I want you … that is, I would ask you … to tell your wife and explain it to her … so she doesn't hear it from someone else and then think that either of us killed him.' He finished baldly. 'Because I didn't kill him, even though I'm not sad he's dead. Anyway, his wife will run it, and she'll be just as bad, you'll see.'

Mamat was momentarily speechless. 'I can tell her about it, but I can't force her to think a certain way. She'll come to her own conclusions. But I'll tell her you told me right away and didn't want to hide it. That's really good.'

Ah Pak nodded, content if not ecstatic. At least he had gotten it off his chest.

# Chapter XII

'Suleiman started this whole thing,' Maryam announced, 'and since he's gone home to Puteh, we've got to speak to both of them.'

Rubiah nodded absently. 'Why did Suleiman start it?'

'Because he got married. That's when everything started to happen.'

'I think it all started with Ruslan, when he lost all his money. That's where Yusuf was going when he was killed. Not to see Suleiman'

'Suleiman set him off,' Maryam dismissed her objections, and Rubiah, as she often did, decided to let it go rather than argue.

Puteh's place was not far from where both Maryam and Rubiah lived, but this was not where the owners of the *kain songket* emporia lived, or even the successful sellers of fabrics. This was smaller, cheaper, flimsier, and Puteh's house, though solid, still gave the impression it might collapse, given an excuse. The house was packed, with seven children and their parents. Suleiman was moping on the front porch, acting the part of an upright citizen home with his family. Puteh, Maryam surmised, was inside cleaning or cooking or caring for the children, which Suleiman would not have seen as his responsibility.

The women hailed him as good neighbours and stood at the bottom of the ladder, watched by several small children distracted by the new arrivals. Suleiman removed the cigarette from his mouth and, acting as a benevolent host, gave them a large smile, beckoning them to climb the ladder and join him on the porch.

'Teh,' he called into the house through the open door, 'look who's come here to see us! Get your mother,' he ordered one of the boys peeking out through a window. He turned and indicated a place for the women to sit. He smiled jovially and produced a package of Rothman's cigarettes, offering some to his guests. How could he afford that, Maryam wondered? She would never allow herself the luxury, though Mamat did, and she was far better off than Suleiman, who was living hand to mouth at best, Perhaps this was part of the whole gambler's attitude: living on dreams and hope rather than on the money you actually had.

Suleiman's wide smile was pasted firmly on his face, overlaying the fear he felt seeing these two prominent *Mak Cik* come to see him. He was no longer a child, he continued to remind himself, and could not be summarily scolded, but part of him dreaded it nevertheless. He believed he could read the judgement in their eyes, that they disapproved of him and all he had done, and his coming back to Puteh was not a mark in his favour, but only the last option of a man at the end of his tether. Reprimanding or not, he could do nothing more than entertain them as best he could. He looked nervously for Puteh, hoping she could carry this off better than he could: they would not consider her at fault.

'When did you get back?' Rubiah inquired sweetly, causing Suleiman to blush bright red and stare at his feet. What did he have that two women wanted him? She couldn't imagine.

'Yesterday,' he mumbled, thinking the lecture was now at hand.

Rubiah would not be constrained by decency. 'So, you left Khatijah now?'

He nodded cautiously, unwilling to set her off.

'And Puteh's taken you back?'

'What else can I do with seven children?' Puteh answered spiritedly as she walked out the door. 'They need a father.' Even this one, she implied, but it remained unsaid. '*Mak Cik*, let me get you something. You must be hot! Come, don't sit in the sun, cool off in the shade.'

She shooed them over to a shady corner as if they were well-dressed chickens, giving her husband a look clearly ordering him out of the way. He sloped out of the shade into the less desirable sun, squinting against the light while trying to seem soigné. Puteh gave rapid-fire orders to her oldest daughter, then turned amiably back to her guests.

'So nice to see you.'

'And you too, and I'm happy it's in better times,' Rubiah said with a significant look towards the lightly sweating Suleiman. 'I can't tell you how glad I am to see that everything is back to normal.'

Puteh smiled and shrugged. What can you do, she implied,

when you're already graced with seven children and no income? At least with him back, it was always possible he might make some money and actually bring it home.

'We got married again yesterday.'

'I couldn't leave my family, I realized that,' Suleiman interjected with a note of pride, even though Maryam and Rubiah believed it was probably Khatijah who realized that, not him. Nevertheless, someone had realized it and acted upon it, and it was all for the better.

But enough chitchat, Maryam thought, once the tea and cookies had arrived and Puteh graciously put forth the best the house had to offer.

'We are here on a delicate matter,' she began, looking earnestly at both her hosts. 'You know *Che* Yusuf has been killed, and, of course, we must speak to everyone who knew him … professionally.'

She wasn't at all sure this was really what she meant: after all, professional seemed to imply someone far more accomplished than Yusuf, but she was loathe to immediately jump into the problems of gambling. 'I know you knew him well, and had for several years,' she said neutrally to Suleiman, 'so I wanted to ask you about him.'

Suleiman sat silent, smoking his cigarette, his shoulders slightly hunched as though expecting a good dressing-down.

'Suleiman?' Rubiah prompted him, hoping he would begin on his own. He looked up, startled. 'Oh! Yes! Yes, I mean, I did know him. Of course.' He smiled all around, and Puteh looked quite murderous as she considered him.

'You spent a lot of time at his place.'

'Yes.'

'Did you often win?' Rubiah asked, cutting through any politeness.

'Sometimes,' said Suleiman. 'No,' said Puteh at the same time.

'Where did you get the money to gamble?'

Perhaps it was none of her business (though Maryam did not consider anything to fall into that category), but she was so curious!

'I work,' Suleiman said defensively.

Puteh snorted. 'He works as a porter sometimes at the market. Not that often, though.'

'And then you use it to gamble.'

'No! I use it to support my family!' he cried. 'I don't spend it all on myself.'

'Most of it,' Puteh corrected him. 'His parents give us money sometimes.' There was a world of hurt, disappointment and humiliation in that sentence.

'So tell me,' Maryam leaned over and dropped her voice, 'did you ever owe *Che* Yusuf a lot of money? Did he ever try to collect from you?'

Suleiman stared at the floor, but Puteh grew scarlet with indignation. 'All my jewelry! All my gold bangles! Not that I had such a large collection,' she admitted, 'but it was mine! And I had to give it to him so he wouldn't beat Suleiman.' Her colour had not subsided.

'Maybe I should have kept them,' she spat, 'and just let him do what he wanted. We had to pay up. I mean, we knew what would happen if we didn't. Maybe even the children would be hurt. I don't know. All my jewelry, and a small piece of land Suleiman inherited. Coconuts. Anything we had we didn't actually have to eat.' She closed her eyes and took deep breaths to calm herself down.

'Is that how Yusuf worked?' Maryam asked. 'Finding the people who had something, anything at all, and then letting them get in deeper and deeper until he could take it all from you?'

Puteh nodded. 'I don't think he'd let you run up too much of a debt if he didn't think you had something he could use. He was smart that way. And mean.'

Suleiman tried feebly to protest, but Puteh overruled him immediately. 'You think he was a nice man? You think he was forgiving? He knew you were weak and he used it to get anything we had. But you gave him the opportunity.' She glared at him and he shrank back. 'And,' she added venomously, 'he introduced him to Khatijah.'

'He had nothing to do with that,' Suleiman cried, stung. 'No one introduced us. She was just … there. And anyway, it's over and I'm back. Aren't you happy about that? That I came back, to take care of you and the children?'

'Are you taking care of us,' she asked ominously. 'You're in charge now?' Her voice had been rising as she spoke, and she suddenly became aware she was now audible to many of her neighbours, and she dropped it to a low growl, which Maryam thought was even more intimidating than a shout.

'Then maybe you should go to work. Because you can't go back to gambling, even if *Cik* Noriah opens the place again. You have nothing! We have nothing! And no one will let you run up a debt without any land to give away. You realize that, don't you.'

With great effort, Puteh calmed herself into silence, though she was still breathing heavily. Maryam pitied her and the burden of anger she so clearly held. It would be so hard to get rid of, and it was deserved. She wondered how Puteh would ever be able to live contentedly with Suleiman after all this. It didn't seem as though she had many options either.

# Chapter XIII

Ruslan had died in a particularly nightmarish way, alone and terrified. He lay forlorn in a stand of rubber trees off the main road between Tumpat and Pengkalan Kubur, across the river and north of Kota Bharu, almost to the border with Thailand. How he got there was anyone's guess; certainly no one was looking for him there, so far from his home, and it was only by chance that a man tapping rubber happened to notice an unfamiliar heap through the trees.

His body, now a bloodless husk, had been dragged to a darker corner from closer to the road, a corner bordering on some vacant land returning to secondary jungle. It was not near any homes or villages, just an empty stretch of road, desolate as only roads can be when even their destinations aren't much to visit.

And Ruslan had not died easy. He was huddled on his side, his arms wrapped around his knees. He was pale, almost translucent, and all his blood had leaked into the dark ground around him, leaving little trace of where it had once been. Ruslan's throat had been torn out, leaving a gaping hole in his neck and shoulder where the blood had poured from him, and the expression on his face would give the man who found him nightmares for the rest of his life.

'We've had tigers here,' that same man explained to Osman after he'd examined the body. Osman thought he'd become hardened during his years in Kelantan when murders seemed to blossom in gay profusion compared to the time before he'd arrived. But this face! The poor soul must have been petrified to see his death rushing towards him.

'Not always regular tigers,' the man continued, eyeing Osman warily. He was a poor man, his sarong well-worn, his T-shirt ragged around the seams. The house couldn't be seen from the road, it was farther in through the trees. It seemed a lonely spot, and Osman wondered why anyone would live so far from other people.

The man appeared to read his mind. 'It's the only land we own,' he explained, watching Osman take in the area. 'My wife wants to move back to Pengkalan Kubur, but I said no, we need to be out here to keep on eye on our rubber. I don't mind it myself, but she gets nervous at night, you see, when it's so dark. We hear tigers sometimes. Not regular ones,' he repeated significantly. Osman realized he was being prodded to ask.

'Regular tigers?'

The man's voice dropped. '*Hala*, were-tigers,' he explained. 'There are people around here who become tigers, they change into tigers and hunt at night. In the morning, they change back into people. I don't like to go in there,' he indicated the heavy growth at the back of the stand of rubber trees. He looked intently at Osman, as if to judge whether to tell him the rest of the story. It seemed he thought the police could handle the truth. 'They have a village: the houses are made of human bones and the roofs of human hair.' He nodded. 'All the were-tigers, you see. Families of them.'

'No wonder your wife is afraid,' Osman commented. 'What about your kids? Aren't you worried the tigers might go after them?'

'Of course, I'm worried,' he answered indignantly. 'I'm their father! What do you think? What can I do? This is where we live.'

Osman nodded. 'And you think it was one of these tigers …?'

'Who else?' The man lit the cigarette Osman offered him and leaned against one of his trees. 'Did you see his throat? Do you think a man did it with his teeth?'

'But it could be a natural tiger, or a dog maybe.' Osman would not accept a supernatural out if a natural suspect could be identified.

The man shrugged. 'If you think so,' he said doubtfully. He drew circles in the dirt with his foot and admired them. 'Maybe where you're from, there aren't any *hala*, I don't know.' He disavowed knowledge of wherever it was Osman called home; somewhere on the west coast, it would seem by his accent. 'Here we have them, and people who have the *hala* spirit, tiger spirit, even if they don't look like tigers. Maybe you don't know about that.' He indicated the marks showing where Ruslan's body had been dragged. 'Something very strong brought him here and hid him so he could come back later and eat him. Tigers do that:

people or animals.'

'I don't see any tiger tracks,' Osman mused.

'You don't see any footprints either,' the man pointed out. 'There aren't any tracks at all. And all the blood is gone.' He shrugged. '*Hala* are strong, and violent, I'm telling you. When they take their tiger form, I think they're stronger than even the real tigers, and more vicious. It's because they have to hide their tiger nature during the day,' he explained quietly. 'So when they become tigers, they're finally themselves. It's the hiding themselves that makes them all the more fierce. You don't have to believe me. You'll find out for yourself who did it.'

Alone with the dead, Osman wondered whether someone collecting gambling debts would send such a bloody message, or if they would disguise it in such horrifying garb. Wouldn't it be better to make it clear to any other gamblers considering flight from non-payment to know who'd killed him, rather than have rumors spread (as surely they would) that there were were-tigers abroad in Tumpat district? The whole point to the death, if indeed it was gambling-related, would be to clearly state that debts must be paid. This corpse stated nothing clearly except that the death was chilling and bloody. But there was no mention, symbolically or otherwise, of accounts yet unclosed.

The Tumpat Police Chief, *Che* Harun, ambled over, keeping his distance from the corpse and remaining in the full light of the road. He had called Osman upon realizing he had a dead body on his hands: better that the Chief of Police in Kota Bharu handle it than it land on Tumpat's desk. And Osman, for his part, assumed the corpse to be Ruslan, for how many men did he have missing?

'Any clues?'

'That fellow there thinks it's a were-tiger.'

Harun nodded solemnly. 'It could be. Look at the wound.'

'Couldn't it be just a regular tiger? Or a dog?'

Harun was noncommittal. 'Maybe.'

'Are there a lot of were-tigers around here?'

Harun was now cautious. 'I don't really know. You know, if they don't do anything like this, then they could be around, but you wouldn't know it. I mean, when it's a human, how would you recognize it?'

He warmed to his topic: he'd been thinking about it since he'd seen Ruslan's corpse. 'If you catch them when they're turning from tiger to man, of course, you'll know. My cousin said he'd seen one early in the morning, before *subuh* once, and his legs were still tiger's legs and he had a tail, but his face and arms were already becoming human. He was standing under his house, waiting to change back completely before going home.

'Some families run them,' he continued, looking off into the distance. 'Though I would think, looking at the body, that when the *hala* changed back, he'd still be all bloody, and would have to wash. Too bad it didn't happen this morning, we could find whoever bathed so early.' Looking at Osman's face, he realized this was the wrong approach to take.

'But of course,' he backtracked, 'there might not be any *hala*. I've never actually caught one.' He assumed an expression of benign neutrality.

Osman began venting his frustration. 'This is a vicious killing. Whoever did this needs to be brought to justice. I don't want to see anything like this ever again.' He quickly realized what he had just said did nothing to disprove the were-tiger theory, which only increased his annoyance.

'You've never seen anything like it,' he told Azrina later that evening. 'I don't even want to describe it to you.'

'You should!' she said stoutly, 'perhaps I can help you. Or at least listen to you,' she amended demurely. She was itching to hear the details, and yet Osman would insist the delicacy of her soul might not withstand the horrors he could relate. She in turn believed she could withstand them with more fortitude than he could, but a frontal assault on his ego was likely to end badly, so she instead launched a determined end run.

'You can't carry this all by yourself,' she began sweetly. 'That's why you have a wife! To help you. To share with you. You worry too much about protecting me and not enough about caring for yourself.' She dropped her eyes momentarily, and then brought them up to look deeply into his. A small, tremulous smile appeared, and Osman swooned – figuratively.

'Ina, you wouldn't believe it. It does look like a tiger attacked him. It took out his whole throat, there's no blood left in him at all!' At this, Azrina did seem to pale somewhat, but Osman had the bit between his teeth and continued unperturbed. 'He looked terrified. Just terrified. And whoever, or whatever, did it then dragged him through the trees to the back of the plot near the jungle. I tell you, I almost thought of a tiger myself, but it's too much of a coincidence: a man with large gambling debts goes missing and then gets conveniently eaten by a tiger. I don't believe it.'

'You're right, it would be too neat. Someone wants him dead. But the message …,' she said thoughtfully. Though she had no experience with the Underworld, she'd read enough crime fiction to know about the meaning of murder, and if there was a code here, it was pretty murky. Underworld denizens, she knew, were not the subtlest of readers, and she surmised any message sent to them would need to be clear and unmistakable. Without tigers of any kind.

'What was he doing up there, anyway?' she asked.

'I have no idea,' Osman answered morosely. 'There isn't anything around there: no village, no nothing. Just these rubber trees.'

'Was he running away?'

'That's what I think, but I still can't get it clear. Why there?'

'Was he coming back from Tak Bai?' she asked, naming the closest Thai town to Pengkalan Kubur.

Osman looked at her thoughtfully, and then slowly started to smile.

# Chapter XIV

Azmi's wedding was rapidly approaching, and Maryam felt as though she had done nothing to prepare. Finally, Rosnah had decided on her colours. (Blue and white: Maryam had been doubtful about white, suggesting cream or even light pink, but Rosnah was adamant, in a sweet and apparently pliant way. This was a talent which would stand her in good stead in the years to come, if she was at all interested in getting anything she wanted, which Maryam did not.) Plus, the sky blue *songket* had been woven and made into the wedding dress already. Azmi would be wearing a white *baju melayu* with a light blue songket *kain selamping* around his waist to keep to the motif. He wisely kept away from the planning and offered his opinion on the proceedings only to agree heartily with whatever Rosnah suggested. Another ability likely to foster future happiness.

Aliza, whose hair had been shaved off due to a head injury the year before, now sported a thick, shiny bob, hanging fashionably to her shoulders, showing off the natural curl. She had grown into a lovely young woman, rivaling her older sister Ashikin, a renowned beauty throughout Kota Bharu. Even as a young mother of one with another child due in two months, Ashikin still turned heads on the street. Aliza had never considered herself in the same league as her sister (and her sister certainly never considered anyone in the same league as herself), but watching Aliza one day, Mamat was surprised to see she was as beautiful as Ashikin, though no one else seemed to notice.

He pointed it out to Maryam, who agreed with him and noted Ashikin had been so widely acknowledged as peerless for so long, it no longer seemed possible for anyone to match her. And since Aliza had grown up believing Ashikin was prettier, it did not occur to her that she'd arrived. Plus, Maryam concluded, if it didn't occur to Aliza, it would never occur to anyone else either. She tasked Mamat with bringing this to Aliza's attention and perhaps guiding her to the realization of how she really looked. Maryam had wedding plans to finalize and could not now undertake self-esteem training.

Yi had entered a gangly stage. Clearly never going to challenge either of his sisters for best looking in the family, he did have a kind of goofy charm Maryam hoped might attract girls looking for more than just a handsome face. He was too young to consider marriage yet, but as a mother, it never hurt to consider the possibilities early. He was due to enter secondary school next year, and was really no longer a baby, but as *bongsu,* the youngest, he was inclined to be indulged and perhaps (only perhaps) acted a bit younger than he was – at least at home.

The wedding itself – that is, the *bersanding,* the sitting-in-state where the bride and groom sit before their guests in their finest *songket* amidst as much decoration as the family can provide – would be held at Rosnah's family's house in Kuala Kelantan, a small *kampong* where the Kelantan River met the sea. Preparations had reached the level of frantic: the main room of the house had been cleared of all its former furniture and the thrones where the bride and groom would sit were placed on a dais, which they had begun festooning with *songket*, lights, flowers and paper ornaments. Almost all Rosnah's female relatives, and the majority of Azmi's, were involved in the redecoration: Aliza, Ashikin and Rubiah's daughters had sat for hours weaving paper wreaths and stringing them with lights, committed to giving Azmi and Rosnah the most beautiful *bersanding* possible, and preserving family honor in so doing. Rubiah made cakes with a single-minded focus which in a lesser woman might have unhinged reason. But really, how could anyone else provide sweets for Rubiah's own family?

Azmi's mood rose on the eve of his wedding, as it seemed his whole life spread before him in a pattern of love and contentment. He could hardly wait for children. But first, the ordeal of the wedding itself loomed, and Rosnah was placed under the care of a *Mak Andam*, a wedding expert, who guided the bride and groom through the intricacies of the Malay traditional wedding. The *Mak Andam* took over everything, including the bride, and Azmi prayed it was temporary and the Rosnah he decided to marry would return to him after the wedding.

He consulted his father on the issue. Mamat rolled his eyes and sighed, remembering his own trial by fire, and assured him even Maryam had become slightly mad for a few weeks before the big day, only to return to earth as soon as it was over and she was no longer encased in *songket*. It would happen to Rosnah as well, Mamat assured him.

'No one's died of a wedding yet,' Mamat intoned gravely.

After the wedding, when the whole family returned to the world normal people inhabit, Maryam noticed all Kelantan buzzed with news of the were-tiger. How she had not tracked on this was hard to fathom, but she had the best excuse imaginable: it was hard to see anything outside the ceremony.

Though Osman tried to keep it quiet, everyone who'd seen the corpse, police and civilian alike, found it impossible not to tell whoever they knew about the attack. Speculation was rampant, and people were frightened. Osman could not at first seriously credit a *hala* as the cause of Ruslan's death, but as he got further away from the initial shock, he found himself thinking more about the creature as something real. After all, he had been unable to construct an alternate theory of death, save for a real tiger, which was not much less frightening than what people believed: it did no good at all to say it wasn't a *hala*, it was a real tiger, a man-eating tiger, now roaming the Tumpat district ready to cause more mayhem. He believed he would cause less panic, though not much less, with the were-tiger theory.

He struggled to explain this to Maryam and Mamat after dinner at their house. (Though Mamat was not completely attentive: the big competition was only two days away, and he feared the unfamiliar company might upset the birds. He was overruled: the birds had to sing in front of plenty of unfamiliar people at the contest, so in fact, this was excellent training, and Mamat should have been grateful that she took it upon herself to acclimate the doves to a strange audience. Mamat knew when he had lost).

Maryam wanted to know more about this story, which seemed so very improbable on the face of it, and what better way than to interrogate Osman in her own living room? When she began her questioning, Azrina moved in closer to make sure she missed nothing.

He told her what he had seen, and both she and Azrina shivered.

'His throat really torn out?' she asked him.

He nodded. 'A huge hole in his neck down to his shoulder. It looked as though it had been ripped out, like with teeth. It wasn't done with a knife.' He shook his head.

'The man who found him told me he thought it was a *hala*, that there was a village of them in the jungle nearby.' Before he'd seen this corpse, he might have laughed afterward at the absurdity of it, but now, having seen what he'd seen, there was no levity.

'I didn't believe him, of course. I mean, villages of were-tigers? With houses made of bone? No, I can't believe anything like that. Can you?' he asked, curious.

Maryam shook her head, but not emphatically. 'Villages? I don't really believe that. And I'm not sure about were-tigers either, but people say …' She trailed off.

'What? What do they say?' Azrina prompted her.

'You hear stories about were-tigers, that certain families run were-tigers, and they're perfectly normal during the day, then go out hunting at night. But before we take on *hala* spirits, isn't it a coincidence that someone who's mixed up in this murder turns up dead? If he owed a lot of money, which he did,' she tapped her cigarette against the stamped tin ashtray, 'then it seems an amazing coincidence that a were-tiger would kill him to collect a debt.' She looked innocently at Osman, as if expecting elucidation.

'It does seem …'

'So, we'll need to speak to *Cik* Noriah again.' She turned to Azrina, who was listening so hard she nearly vibrated. 'If she's already spoken to someone about collecting debts owed to Yusuf …'

'You don't think she …'

'Is a *hala*?' Maryam finished for him. 'Very unlikely. I've never heard any talk about it, and there surely would be if she were hunting in Kampong Penambang.'

'No!' Osman blushed at being so toyed with. 'I mean, do you think she's already talked to someone about collecting her debts? It's so soon after Yusuf's death.'

'She isn't that sentimental,' Maryam told him drily. 'I don't doubt she's getting to work right away. She can't afford to have her debtors relax and spend their money somewhere else.' She thought of Zainuddin, already counting on his debt disappearing. Bad for business; even she knew that.

'Can I come with you?' Azrina asked suddenly, shy at the thought of her own temerity, but so very anxious to come along. 'I could help you.'

'Oh, I don't know,' Maryam began, her eyes trained on Osman.

'*Sayang,* do you really think it's a good idea?' he asked.

She nodded. 'Let's talk about it later,' he advised her, reluctant to have this discussion in front of Maryam, who looked happily amused. She took pity on him, and led the conversation around to other topics.

The day of the competition finally dawned, though Mamat had already been awake for hours, sitting on the porch murmuring to Borek. Maryam woke and began preparing coffee and breakfast, though she knew Mamat wouldn't be able to eat anything. The birds, however, showed no signs of performance anxiety and ate everything put in front of them.

'See how calm they are?' Mamat told her. 'That's good, that's excellent. It means they'll do well today.'

'Of course, they will,' she agreed heartily. 'I think they'll do beautifully. What does Ah Pak say? Does he think they could be winners?'

He nodded, suddenly remembering his last conversation with his friend. What was it he had wanted Mamat to tell Maryam? In his pre-competition excitement, he couldn't recall. Maybe afterward it would come to him. He turned back to his mashed banana and ginger, feeding his birds from his hand. Maryam sat with him on the porch and helped, calming the birds, though in truth they didn't seem to need it as much as Mamat, and making sure they had enough to eat. They packed the birds in their cages, hanging two from the handles of the motorbike, with Maryam sitting side-saddle with Borek's cage on her lap. Mamat drove very slowly and carefully through a just waking Kota Baru, towards the field in Kubang Kerian with its circle of tall poles.

Ah Pak was waiting for them, like a boxing coach with his prize contender. He hurried over to Mamat, gently helped Maryam off the motorbike and took the cage from her. Maryam was amused that he seemed to actually be helping Borek off the seat rather than her, but this was, after all, a gathering of people mad for *merbok*. She followed them dutifully, though neither man was aware of her existence, or actually, any existence outside of the birds.

They crouched together, their heads touching, under the pole Ah Pak had already chosen as the most auspicious, due to the direction the cage would face and the exact mix of sun and shade it offered. Maryam had little understanding of the minutiae of positioning the birds, and less interest. She personally believed it made no difference at all, but that men made their hobby as complicated as possible in order to look thoughtful and knowledgeable when they discussed it in front of other people. She herself would have chosen whichever pole was closer and offered the most shade for her, not the bird.

After the birds had been introduced to the area, and their spirits revived with *air halia*, or ginger water, Ah Pak wandered away from Mamat and found Maryam. With a large smile pasted onto his round and friendly face, he tried to tamp down his anxiety, though Maryam sensed it anyway and was puzzled. He squatted down next to her in the shade and examined the dirt at his feet.

'I think Borek has a good chance of winning,' he began. Maryam nodded pleasantly. 'Has Mamat spoken to you? About me, I mean?' Maryam shook her head and tried to look encouraging. Ah Pak sighed regretfully; it meant he now had to bring up the topic by himself, which embarrassed him. He shot Mamat a reproving look, but Mamat wasn't even looking at him, so it had no effect whatsoever.

'It's about Yusuf.' He took a deep breath and spoke the rest as quickly as he could while still remaining intelligible.

'Do you know my oldest son, Kit Siang? A good boy, but as boys do, he fooled around for a little while. You remember how Azmi was before he joined the army. And now look at him!'

Ah Pak and his family had been to Azmi's wedding, and had seen what a respectable young man he'd grown into. Maryam nodded, as she remembered Azmi's wild days all too well, and the endless worry they had given her. Of course, it wasn't serious trouble, she assured herself, just the usual adolescent card playing and occasional beer drinking, which was now completely over. But still …

'So you see, Kit Siang was doing some gambling. It would have been nothing, an unimportant indulgence, but Yusuf let it get out of hand, and he ran up a lot of losses. Yusuf should have cut him off early, after all, he knew he was just a kid, but he also knew I'd pay up, so he just let him continue. After the first time, I spoke to him and told him not to do it again, but you know how boys can be. Kit Siang went back and Yusuf let it go a second time. I was really angry then.'

Maryam couldn't really imagine Ah Pak angry, as he always looked so amiable. But then, of course, fathers got angry when protecting their children. Even the mild-mannered Mamat was moved to rage when dealing with Azmi. She prayed Yi would be different.

'I thought, I know … I mean, I still …' He began again.

'Yusuf was just draining me. He knew I'd never let Kit Siang get hurt for not paying his debts. You know, *Kakak*, Yusuf had ways of collecting that I could never let happen to my son. His mother would kill me,' he added thoughtfully, and Maryam wondered which he feared more: Yusuf hurting his son or his wife hurting him.

'So,' he said, summing up his confession, 'I just wanted to make sure you knew. I mean, knew I had dealings with Yusuf, and Kit Siang and the whole story from me, not because you discovered it somewhere and wondered why I hadn't told you.' He looked up at her and Maryam felt for him.

'I'm very glad you told me. Thank you, *Abang*. And Kit Siang, where is he now?'

'He's staying with my sister in Gua Musang. I have three of them there, and they're looking for a good wife for him. They've been sending candidates to my wife,' he smiled, jolly again. 'They'll find one, believe me.' Maryam did. 'He'll settle down, come back to Kota Bharu and work with me. He already told me his wild days are over,' Ah Pak said with some satisfaction. 'He finally realized his own mistake.' He smiled at Maryam again. 'Finally.'

'I know what you mean,' she agreed with him. 'When did he go down?'

Here Ah Pak was slightly more vague. 'A little while ago, when his mother lost all patience with him.' He nodded and rose, looking far happier than he had when he first came over to her, and returned back to Mamat, who had barely noticed he'd been gone.

The murmuring of the coaches became louder as the field became more crowded, and some birds even burst into short snatches of song. The sun was nowhere near full strength, but it was now truly morning and no longer dawn, and the judge made his appearance.

He was a local notable who had been a contestant for years, and a famed breeder of *merbok*. Now, however, he had retired from competition and become more religious in his old age. As a judge, he had now assumed a loftier position, removed from the actual gambling. He made a slow, deliberate circuit of the ring, looking over all the contestants as their owners showed them off to best advantage. Final sips of water given, the last bite of a special meal, home-brewed vitamins, or just the fluffing of feathers, and then the contest began.

The birds in their cages were hoisted like flags to the tops of the poles and entreated to sing, with the soft calling of their names, or encouraging words, or even silent prayer. Mamat made a whirring sound usually betokening their meals and grooming while Maryam took over the prayers. For a moment or two, the birds were silent, as though they had decided as a group to boycott the activity, but then they began full-throated singing, each apparently inspiring the others. The judge stood for a few minutes under each pole, concentrating on listening only to the bird above him. Mamat looked serious and completely enraptured by the barrage of song around him. Maryam watched him anxiously as he stood below Borek, their prize bird and best chance for winning. She could tell nothing from the impassive face of the judge, who acknowledged none of the people at all, lest he be accused of favouritism.

Mamat was sweating slightly, and his hands trembled just a little. He was so nervous, Maryam longed to take him in her arms and try to calm him, or at least provide some comfort. But it was unthinkable for a couple to do anything like that in public, so she contented herself with a warm and, she hoped, encouraging smile. In his anxiety, he seemed to look right through her, and did not acknowledge her smile, or even her presence. While she hated to see him so overwrought, she did secretly think he might have been overdoing it, and perhaps it would be more seemly for a man his age to keep some emotion in check and remain even a little more impassive. Mamat could usually do this with no problem, but such was his identification with his birds that right now, he was incapable of showing anything but his rawest feelings, like a child ready to cry.

Ah Pak clapped a hand on Mamat's shoulder in encouragement. From the look on his face, Maryam gathered he thought the judges had liked Borek and might actually award him the top prize.

Mamat looked beyond speech, shooting imploring looks at the judge, who noticed no being who didn't have wings. Now, all the coaches were milling around the field, watching the judge and each other; the professional handlers were crowding together to discuss their clients; while the owners, like Mamat, were more emotionally involved in the process. Maryam could not abandon their other birds and go to Mamat, so she retreated into the shade, and watched him talk to Ah Pak, clearly going over every move of the judge, every note sung by Borek.

At last, the judge turned to the expectant crowd, which immediately fell silent. He gestured to two birds – Borek and another who had been shown by a professional handler. Mamat looked stunned, and then deliriously happy. He tried to keep himself in check, to maintain a dignified mien, but could not even tone down his smile. It appeared Borek came in first! Maryam had hoped for it but not dared to believe it, and now it was true. Ah Pak smiled and giggled, shaking Mamat's shoulder and gesticulating wildly. Maryam thought her husband might just levitate. It was amazing: he had won.

# Chapter XV

Maryam had been regaled that night at least seven times (by her own count) with the full story of the competition, and was up until all hours reliving the fateful moment when the judge announced his decision. She could not deny Mamat the pleasure of relating it. By midnight, he'd already worn out Rubiah and Abdullah, Malek and Zahara, and even Aliza and Yi. Ashikin and Daud had come over to hear of the triumph and congratulate the victor, and for the first time in her young life, Nuraini was not the centre of her grandfather's universe. She did not take it well. As Maryam sought to comfort her, she acknowledged that Nuraini was indeed her mother's child. The immanent arrival of a younger sibling promised to be a challenge.

Mamat was close to flying from pure happiness: his first big-time competition, and he'd won. He knew Borek could do it; he'd listened to his song long enough to see he was a champion and more than ready to compete all over Kelantan. (This concerned Maryam somewhat, as she wasn't sure how far she cared to travel with birds, but surely now was not the time to debate it. Now was the time to nod vigorously and exclaim 'I know!' in tones of ringing confidence, which she did).

After everyone left, it was really not that far from the time she'd be rising for work, so she willed her eyes wide open and listened again, trying for the same level of enthusiasm she'd felt eight hours earlier. It was indeed a *tour de force* of wifely solicitude.

At last, lying down in silence, surrounded by the dark in which her facial expression could be neither seen nor interpreted, Maryam allowed her mind to drift back to Ah Pak's surprising confession – if that, indeed, was what it was.

Without doubt, there was more to it than Ah Pak cared to tell, and his genial insistence that Kit Siang had gone to Gua Musang only to assume the mantle of maturity was ridiculous. He could do that right here in Kota Bharu under the watchful eyes of his parents instead of travelling down to what could only be described as the middle of nowhere under the supervision of his aunts. Maryam sniffed; there were plenty of eligible Chinese girls right here in coastal Kelantan if you were looking for a wife.

No, Kit Siang was shipped out to keep him far away from an investigation, Maryam was convinced. She didn't know whether he was a material witness or an actual suspect, but in either event, he'd best return home and face the police – and Maryam, perhaps even more forbidding for him – sooner rather than later. She decided to approach Ah Pak with her conclusions the next day, and hoped he would accept it rationally.

The next morning, Mamat was no less transported and left early for Ah Pak's store so they could review every second together in real time. Maryam went to the market, now exhausted, and revived herself upstairs with Rubiah's coffee and just a few pieces of cake. She told Rubiah everything Ah Pak had said to her, and Rubiah immediately agreed with her conclusions.

'You should talk to Osman,' she advised, 'and let him get Kit Siang back to Kota Bharu. After all, you can hardly go all the way down to Gua Musang and bring him back by the ears.'

That was an interesting possibility, and worth contemplating, but Rubiah was right. Besides, a summons to return ahead of schedule to Kota Bharu would no doubt be read as a threat, and the entire extended family would rally around Kit Siang to keep him away from the authorities. It would have to be done more circuitously.

# Chapter XVI

Maryam walked quickly through Kampong Penambang, anxious to reach home after a long and frustrating day. The market had been packed, which ought to have been cause to rejoice, but it seemed as though every time-wasting, tight-fisted tourist had been there, all looking to stroke the fabric and ask a million questions without buying. These were the worst kind of would-be customers, devouring all Maryam's reserves of good will and patience while offering nothing in return. And the investigation seemed stalled as well. What she had assumed would be a straightforward case, with a wastrel gambler of unimpeachable guilt clearly identified, had instead assumed large and amorphous proportions, where everyone, and no one, looked guilty. She berated herself for volunteering to solve this crime: it was as clear a case of overreaching pride as she had ever seen, and she had no one to blame but herself.

A long talk with Rubiah had not really made her feel better, though Rubiah was very sympathetic and was, indeed, involved in it herself. But even turning over and re-examining all the evidence had not brought them any closer to finding the killer, or killers, for now they had two bodies, so both the crimes and the suspects were multiplying.

As she hurried along, she thought she heard something off to her right, behind a house which stood dark and silent. Her imagination, already geared up by her discussion with Rubiah, worked overtime, and she refused to feed the fire any longer.

But the soft padding did not fade, nor at first did it appear to come closer, but rather, it remained off to the side, keeping pace with her, stopping when she did to look fearfully over her shoulder. This was, after all, Kampong Penambang, she reminded herself: her home for all her life, where she knew every house and every winding path, and she knew without doubt the direction from which she heard the noise was not an open field but houses with people, though she could see no lights. It was not so late that all the village should lay quiet. People in Kelantan went to sleep late and rose early, and at this time, she should have still heard the voices of her neighbours, or a television, or at least seen a light. But as though under a spell, it was both completely dark and silent. There was not even a moon.

And suddenly, there beside her, she felt – rather than saw – the tiger. Felt the heat from its body and its unmistakable wild animal smell, which raised the hair on the back of her neck. And the sound! A low rumble in the back of its enormous throat. The tiger swung its head – strong, large, rippled with muscle – under Maryam's trembling hand, as though asking her to pet him. He could easily have torn her apart, yet he stood quietly next to her, placing the flat of his head against her, purring. She felt a surge of kinship with the tiger and was no longer frightened. He had come to tell her something; she could feel the tiger's desire to communicate with her, to warn her. They stood together, their hearts beating in unison, for what seemed like several minutes and, suddenly, the spell was over.

The tiger pulled away from her and roared at the top of his voice, answered by shrill screams of terror from the village beasts, from water buffalo to duck, and then he left, disappearing with a swish of his tail into the dark, and not even a single stripe to be seen.

In the morning though, Maryam ran back to where she'd met him, and his huge pug marks were clear in the dirt. But even as she watched, they seemed to smoothen out in the road, like someone straightening a wrinkled sheet, and a sudden, short rain shower wiped everything away.


She sat later on her porch, thoroughly shaken, with the village *bomoh* listening sympathetically and Mamat himself serving cups of tea and cigarettes. Maryam's hand shook as she smoked, and she knew she was repeating herself, but couldn't help it.

'It was warning me,' she insisted, frightened but firm, while the *bomoh* regarded her steadily. 'I don't know what it was telling me, but it came to help me.'

'It's a powerful spirit, the *hala*,' Pak Lah commented. 'It doesn't want to hurt you, or it would have. Look at that poor man near Pengkalan Kubur. This tiger knows you.'

'Do you think it's a real tiger?' Mamat asked.

With a slight smile, Pak Lah shook his head.

'How could it be? There are no tigers here. A real tiger would have killed if it came into a village. Only a were-tiger seeks to talk to us.'

'Who is it?' Maryam asked. 'Is it someone who lives here?'

Pak Lah shrugged. 'I don't know. Maybe it came from up near Tumpat to tell you …'

'Tell me what?'

'You're in danger.'

Maryam nodded. 'I know it came to help me.'

'Can you give us an *azimat*?' Mamat inquired anxiously. 'She needs some protection.'

'Not from *this* tiger.' Maryam surprised them both, and herself, by saying it, but as soon as it was said, she knew it was absolutely true. 'He means me no harm; he wants to help me.'

'He?' asked Mamat.

She nodded. 'It's a man.' She thought for a moment. 'I hope he comes back,' she said, gaining conviction. 'I wish I knew what he wanted to tell me. I feel so stupid.'

Pak Lah rose and stretched his legs. 'You might find out tonight, he might come to you in a dream. But don't go out looking for him,' he admonished her. 'You don't want to count on a were-tiger as a friend. Remember, *adik,* it's a powerful spirit, and it's uncontrolled.'

Maryam nodded absently. 'Are you listening?' Mamat demanded, worried.

'Of course,' she told him. But neither she nor Mamat really

believed it

As the day wore on, she longed to sleep, to meet the tiger again, and perhaps understand what he wanted to say. It was an almost physical longing, and she remembered the feel of his head under her hand, and the sound he made. She wondered at herself, dreaming of tigers; no, dreaming of *that* tiger, and only that one.

And he came to her in a dream, where she stood at the same place she'd stood the night before, but this time, instead of merely sensing him, she saw him. His coat was a shimmering orange, of such a saturated colour it seemed to glow, and his stripes were the complete absence of light. And his head ... such a noble brow, with a neck of solid muscle. It was his eyes, though, that mesmerized her: deep yellow and almost human in their expression. Once again, he stood next to her, leaning his head under her hand, which did not tremble this time, but remained strong and confident, stroking her tiger and talking to it without using her voice.

He replied to her. Indeed, he had come to warn her, to protect her. He would watch over her, he promised, and told her not to fear him. But there were others she should fear, though he could not mention their names directly.

'They are weak, yet they are strong. They throw riches away, yet they collect them. They are despised, yet they are feared.' The tiger now fell silent and, with a long look into her eyes, turned and disappeared.

Maryam awoke, sitting straight up in bed, covered in sweat, trying to scream. Mamat slept quietly beside her, and the *kampong* was peaceful, lit by a nearly full moon to a silvery glow. The visit had not happened in this world, but in a dream. She sat in bed with her head in her hands, fearing she had gone mad.

# Chapter XVII

Her family crowded around her on the verandah, offering advice, all speaking at the same time, plying her with sweet coffee, cakes and cigarettes. In short, they acted just as a family should when one of its beloved members seems to be leaving reality behind. Her brother Malek practically ordered her to stop thinking about tigers, any tigers, and especially talking tigers.

'Yam,' he nearly moaned, 'think about what you're saying! Tigers are talking to you in dreams ... Have some more coffee, it will wake you up.' He turned to Mamat as though passing the baton.

'It's just a dream, Yam,' Mamat said earnestly. 'It doesn't mean a *hala* was really talking to you, just that....Well, of course you dreamed about it, after having such a scare! It was on your mind. It didn't come to you. You must believe me.'

She nodded silently. She must believe him, true, but she didn't. They hadn't seen the tiger, they hadn't heard him. How could they know anything about him, when in fact, she alone knew him?

Concern creased the faces of Malek and Rubiah, and her children looked truly frightened. Maryam realized she needed to at least appear to have forgotten the tiger, and continue on with her investigation, for her children if nothing else. They didn't need a madwoman for a mother. Why, soon she would be as bad as Hamidah, with long ratty hair and unwashed clothes. No, the tiger would remain her secret, and she would not speak of him again. But how then could she tell Rubiah of his riddle and how it would help them identify Yusuf's killer?

She looked thoughtfully over at Rubiah. 'I know you're right. I think maybe I was … upset from yesterday, and so I kept thinking about the tiger.' She sighed. Mamat looked relieved, while Rubiah looked deeply suspicious. 'I don't think I'll see him again.'

She looked down at her sarong, appearing to be absorbed in it. Rubiah stood up, addressing herself to Malek and Mamat.

'I'm going to get Pak Lah. This has gone on long enough.'

'Wait! She sounds a little better,' Mamat said optimistically.

Rubiah snorted at him. 'I know when she's lying. She's going to agree with us so we'll all leave her alone, but really, she'll keep on about this tiger thing in her head, and by the time we all figure it out, it will be too late, and she'll already be too far gone for us to help her. We've got to act now.' With a stern look at her cousin, she marched off the porch in search of Pak Lah.

Maryam didn't dare to look Mamat in the eye, not wanting to see his reaction to her attempted recovery. He looked dejected, while Malek looked irritated.

'Yam,' her brother said slowly, 'I don't know what you're thinking. Maybe Pak Lah can help. I hope so, because I don't know what to do.' Mamat perked up. 'I'm sure …'

'I'm alright,' Maryam assured him. 'I know the tiger didn't – '

She was interrupted by the arrival of a bemused Pak Lah, trailed by an adamant Rubiah. He greeted everyone cordially, then asked Maryam if she would follow him into the front room where they could talk. She rose and entered the house, while everyone watched her.

'What's this I hear?' Pak Lah asked easily, lighting both their cigarettes. 'The tiger came to you in a dream?' Maryam nodded dumbly. 'Your family is afraid you're going mad.'

She nodded again, then burst out, 'I am not, Pak Lah! The tiger came to me in a dream just as you said he might. And he told me ...'

'He talked to you?'

'But not with our voices. I just heard him and he heard me. I can't explain. But he told me he'd protect me, but that other people wished me harm. And then he said some things to lead me to the murderer. He said, "They are weak, yet they are strong. They throw riches away, yet they collect them. They are despised, yet they are feared." I remember exactly what he said, so clearly.'

She looked at him beseechingly, willing him not to think her crazy and dismiss her. Pak Lah looked out onto the porch and pursed his lips in thought.

'*Cik* Rubiah!' he called, and she walked in, looking grim. 'I want you to hear this,' he said softly, and turned again to Maryam, encouragingly. 'Tell her, *adik*, what you just told me.' Maryam complied, and Rubiah answered immediately. 'Din.'

'Din?'

'Din. It's too bad your tiger didn't add "stupid", because then it would be without doubt,' she said acidly. 'Listen to me: he's weak because he gambles and can't control himself, but strong because he's physically strong. He gambles, so he throws riches away, but I can't think of anything for him collecting them. He's got nothing.

'But never mind. Despised, of course, and feared, of course: he's so big and strong and could kill you so easily. If your tiger was really telling you anything,' she continued confidently, 'it's Din.'

Maryam felt her mind moving faster than it had in a long time. 'But it could also be Suleiman. Weak, yes. Strong, I can't think of anything …

'No wait, not Suleiman.' She thought again. 'Ah Pak! Yes! He fits all of it.'

'Despised?' Rubiah asked doubtfully. 'I don't think anyone despises him.'

'Well, maybe it means Chinese in general. You know, lots of people don't like them.' She blushed slightly to have said this so baldly.

'You aren't convinced,' Rubiah admonished her. 'It should come to you immediately when you hear that riddle, not going through your list of suspects and choosing one. However,' Rubiah allowed, 'It does kind of fit Ah Pak.'

Maryam shook her head. 'I can't believe Ah Pak would do something like this.'

'Why not?' Rubiah pursued. 'The man was threatening his

son! Of course, he would protect him.' She took a drag on her cigarette and then examined it between her fingers. 'Anyone would.'

'But murder,' Maryam breathed. 'And then, why would the tiger warn me?' Rubiah rolled her eyes at Pak Lah, but Maryam saw it.

'Stop it. I'm not crazy, no matter what Malek thinks. Or you,' she added with asperity.

'Ah Pak isn't going to hurt me.'

'Are you sure?' Pak Lah asked. 'I know he's a nice man and all that, but might he try?'

'Did the tiger kill Ruslan also?'

Maryam was nonplussed. 'I … I don't know. Why would he?'

Rubiah sighed with exaggerated patience. 'Maryam, either the tiger is watching you and advising you about this case …' Her tone made it clear she did not believe this for a moment. 'Or you aren't talking to tigers at all, which is the better answer.'

Maryam sat silent. If Rubiah, her closest friend, relative and ally doubted her sanity, then perhaps she was mad after all. She rubbed her eyes to clear them.

'Maybe an exorcism. Another *main puteri*…' Pak Lah murmured.

'No!' Maryam surprised them with the vehemence of her denial. 'I won't have *main puteri* done for me every year. I don't need one.'

'Perhaps not,' Pak Lah soothed. 'A *jampi*, perhaps, and a talisman that you can wear. The tiger needs to leave you, *Adik*.

You can't follow him to become a tiger yourself,' he said sadly, as though he knew how very tempting that sounded to Maryam at the moment. 'I know what you're thinking now: '*kukur apa kepada kukur? Nyiur juga yang binasa*': What does the rasp care about rasping? It's the coconut which suffers.

'I know you think it's easy for us to tell you what to do, and to ignore the tiger, but we haven't seen it, have we? We don't know how it feels to see it, and yet we tell you to turn your face away from it.'

He looked at her kindly. 'I've known you a long time, and I can tell you, this tiger will make you mad. A person – I mean a person who is not a *hala* – can't talk to tigers. It will take you with it, Maryam, you will have no choice but to follow it. You can't live in both worlds, and the *hala* world looks very good to you now. But it means you will leave everything of your human life behind.'

Maryam began to be frightened: if it were true, how could she leave her family and everything she knew to follow a tiger? It was insane.

Pak Lah looked deeply into her eyes. '*Seperti kapas dimakan api:* like cotton eaten by fire, you will be completely destroyed. Believe me, Maryam. You're playing with your very life here.'

With a long look at her, Pak Lah rose and walked slowly out to the porch. Rubiah would not leave, but said nothing, merely looking hard at Maryam as though memorizing her features before they were lost. Maryam burst into hysterical tears, afraid to lose her life, but also afraid to lose her tiger.

# Chapter XVIII

Azrina trotted happily behind Maryam and Rubiah as they sauntered to Noriah's house to see how business was doing. The widow had clearly been busy. Workmen were swarming over the old house, enlarging the parlour, adding electricity and running water, and a real stove in the kitchen. It was going to be a first-class institution when Noriah was finished, and they found her standing in front of it, keeping a keen eye on the job.

They greeted each other warmly, and though Maryam and Rubiah could not approve of the use to which the building would be put, as businesswomen they were impressed with the work being done and Noriah's will to improve.

'I'm going to charge them to come inside,' she informed Maryam, gesturing with her cigarette. 'No more deadbeats. I'm making something really nice here, people can come from all over and play, eat, whatever.' Maryam picked up her ears at 'whatever', remembering what Khatijah had told them. Still Noriah chattered on, proud of her project.

'You know, all those people who owed money to Yusuf, I'm not letting them in here. This is for people who can pay their debts. I'm not collecting.' She thought for a moment.

'So much trouble with that, and then, *Kakak*, I'd have to pay someone to get it from them.' (*Beat it out of them, more like*, Maryam thought.) 'So this is for people who have the money to gamble, not the ones who should never have started in the first place.'

This seemed to describe most of Yusuf's clientele, but perhaps Noriah knew other, well-heeled gamblers whose custom she was targeting.

'Will Khatijah be working here?' Maryam asked casually.

Noriah shook her head. 'I think it's time Khatijah and I had some time apart,' she said cryptically.

Azrina edged closer to the group, anxious not to miss a word if that were possible. 'Who's that?' Noriah asked shortly.

Maryam introduced them. 'Ah, this is *Cik* Azrina. Police Chief Osman's wife. She's come from Perak.'

Noriah grunted, not even bothering to feign interest when Azrina smiled eagerly. 'So nice to meet you,' Azrina said.

Noriah looked briefly at her, then looked away. 'Perak?' she said witheringly.

'Yes,' Azrina answered politely.

The corners of Noriah's mouth turned down before she corrected them, and she looked back at the work. 'Two weeks,' she informed Maryam and Rubiah, ignoring Azrina. 'Then it's done.'

'How about the debts *Che* Yusuf was collecting?' Rubiah added. 'Are you forgiving those?'

Noriah snorted. 'Forgiving? No. They'll have to pay me. Everything's going to be settled up before I open this new place.'

'How will you do it?' Maryam asked.

Noriah looked at her, surprised at such an aggressive question. 'I'll just …' She let the rest of her answer fade away as she sought to ignore the question altogether.

'As part of our investigation,' Rubiah reminded her. 'That's why we're asking. Have you hired someone?'

'I'm not doing it myself,' she said, clearly annoyed. 'I'm supervising this,' she said, as though otherwise she'd be stopping by the houses of her debtors and physically threatening them. Maryam doubted it was really a job for a woman, unless it was a really frightening harridan. Noriah turned away from the worksite and began walking over to the village coffee stall. 'Let's have something to drink,' she called to them.


The men came from Thailand, from Patani, and they were Thai, not Malay, and therefore difficult to talk to. Their Malay was basic at best, and for all Noriah knew, so was their Thai; they did not appear much given to, or perhaps even capable of, having a sustained conversation in any language. They were an unsavoury crew, perfectly happy to hurt someone to get what they wanted, not easily swayed by other people's problems. They were difficult to control, understanding, as they did, only force, and if fear wasn't in the mix of their emotions, its place was filled by contempt.

Just before he died, Yusuf had mentioned bringing them to

Kota Bharu for a few days, to 'clean up' the outstanding debts owed to him. He knew them from his whiskey-buying trips, and though it would be greatly overstating the case to say they were friends, you could call them operators with parallel interests: Yusuf's in procuring cheap whiskey, and theirs in making money without much effort. They meshed perfectly, and since their spheres of influence never overlapped, they never had cause to argue.

Noriah's mistake had been inviting them to Kelantan to undertake the clean-up Yusuf had left undone, and she knew it was her decision alone that landed her in her current straits. Her contact in Patani, a Malay 'entrepreneur', had advised her not to do it. 'Once they're in,' he told her, 'you won't get rid of them so easily, and you won't be able to control them.'

When she didn't take his advice, he shrugged, unwilling to really get involved. After all, what had he to gain by it? Any fool could see this would end badly, and if Noriah chose not to recognize it, what could he do? He did as she requested, pocketed his finder's fee, and promptly forgot all about it. And three men, whose very names Noriah could neither pronounce nor remember, came to Kota Bharu to help her.

*Bingong tengkat, cerdik begar:* when stupid, quarrelsome; when clever, difficult. They *were* impossible to control, though they had only just arrived. Noriah could see her initial orientation talk to them was completely ignored and they treated her with little respect. She was now reluctant to give them any information on her debtors, lest they prove both overzealous in intimidating them and extremely lax in turning the funds over to her.

She had realized early on she would have a difficult time collecting, but now felt her solution was worse than her problem. The men would do as they pleased, and possibly walk away with her ill-gotten money, and her only recourse would be to set out a group of other ruffians to keep these in line. The money she would have to disburse to do this, lowlife after lowlife, would bankrupt her, and she wished Yusuf had never mentioned these people. In the end, she decided it was his fault for even starting her down this road and, in fact, he was the one who 'bore responsibility for the sin'

In the face of Maryam's questions, however, Noriah reverted to her first instinct: deny and hope it would all finally work out as she had planned. Although she had wanted them to find Yusuf's killer – or if unable to do that, at least identify someone who could be blamed for it and therefore provide closure – she emphatically did not want them digging into her private business to do so. She had respected Maryam, perhaps even liked her in a disinterested sort of way, as she regarded everyone not directly involved in her business or her family. But now she was angry about Maryam's questions, and began to feel crowded by her. Before Yusuf's death, she would not have taken any action based on this. Perhaps she would mention it to him, and then remain happily ignorant of anything that might happen. Those days, lamentably, were over, and now Noriah had to take care of herself.

As they made themselves comfortable at the small, rickety counter of the local coffee stall, Noriah grandly ordered coffees all around and commandeered whatever cakes were available.

Rubiah was reluctant to lower herself to eat substandard fare – by definition, any not made by her. She poked at the cakes with a doubtful forefinger, shaking her head ever so slightly in dismay at what she saw in front of her. She sighed, nearly silently, but Maryam caught it, as she was supposed to, and realized she, too, could not eat a cake such as this. Noriah did not notice any of this, and tucked happily into the cakes and coffee, while Maryam and Rubiah sipped their coffee in a controlled and refined manner.

'So,' began Maryam, not to be derailed by the promise of food and drink, 'did you hire anyone? I ask because I think, you know, it would be very difficult for a woman to collect. They'd have to be a little afraid of you, wouldn't they? People usually aren't that afraid of women.'

'I don't know about that,' Noriah mused. 'I think we can be … persuasive. I mean, it isn't just threatening to hurt them, you know. They must understand there are consequences for not paying, and they don't have to be a beating.' She stirred the coffee in her cup slowly while watching it.

'Then what?' Maryam asked, truly interested.

'Well, there are the courts.'

'For a gambling debt? Gambling's illegal. You'd get into more trouble than they would,' Rubiah corrected her. 'I don't see the courts as a way. No, I think you have to be able to let them know they'll be hurt,' she concluded, as if considering a career in debt collection herself. Maryam looked at her with wonder, Noriah with something close to hatred.

'You seem to be thinking a lot about it, *Kakak*,' she said, barely controlling her voice. 'Are you interested in taking it up?' She tried for a light tone, but the undertone of anger seeped through.

Rubiah bit her lip to tamp down the flash of annoyance she felt. 'I'm sorry, *Kakak*,' she said, not bothering to make the sentiment believable. 'It's just … well, I was wondering,' and she leaned forward, as if to impart some secret wisdom to her companions. 'It's very difficult trying to do this on your own, collect the old debts, that is. I've heard the late *Che* Yusuf sometimes had to resort to force, and that the people who owed him money knew he'd do that.

'But we women? Who worries about that? And then, too, your debtors are all men, and so you see, I wonder if you'll be forced to bring in people to collect for you, and then you'll have these people here – not nice people, we all know that – and then what? They can collect the debt, but how do you get it from them, you see? It's the same problem as before, but worse, because these men won't care what you think.' She leaned back in her chair, satisfied with her speech. Noriah was red in the face, and apparently rendered speechless.

Maryam smiled approvingly and took a dainty sip of her coffee, patted her lips with a tiny napkin, and prepared to leave. 'Thank you for the coffee and your time, *Cik* Noriah,' she said primly, as though she wasn't speaking to someone from Kampong Penambang at all, but a stranger met at an official function. She took Azrina's arm as they left, as if to guide her down a slippery path, when it was only a typical dirt lane of her village. As they left, Noriah considered whether Rubiah actually knew about the men from Thailand, or was it so obvious everyone would guess and not wonder at all when she reaped the whirlwind she had wrought. She wanted to moan and put her head in her hands, but instead glared at the owner of the stall, startling him, and stalked off back to her house, furious at everyone she knew.

# Chapter XIX

Kit Siang was subdued when he returned from Gua Musang, and it was not just because he was attaining maturity and acquiring a wife. It was a motorcade which deposited him back at his family home, with a line of black cars holding his aunts, their husbands and children, his bride-to-be and her entire family. Kit Siang was not entirely sure there wasn't at least one other person he *didn't* know who somehow hitched a ride to Kota Bharu, but what did that matter?

After welcoming his guests, his father quickly drew him into a private room for an urgent talk. Ah Pak had noticed the Thai thugs Noriah had imported, and knew immediately there would be trouble with them – at least for Noriah if no one else. He was sorry for her, finding herself in that kind of situation, for it was easy to call these people down from Patani, but quite another thing to send them back. And though neither Ah Pak nor his son owed Noriah anything now, he feared that in the future, his son might be tempted to visit Noriah's new gambling palace and place himself squarely in the hands of these men.

(And he wasn't even sure about present debts, though he

devoutly hoped Kit Siang had not done anything remarkably stupid before he was whisked down to Ulu Kelantan). He could at least talk to Yusuf; he doubted very much the same could be said of this far less communicative group.

The Kit Siang he sent down to Gua Musang would have bristled at the suggestion he stay away from all forms of gambling for the time being and might have argued with his father, or withdrawn into sullen silence which presaged his doing exactly what he wanted to as soon as his father was out of earshot. This Kit Siang showed no signs at all of disapproval, but nodded his head quietly as Ah Pak explained the situation to him, and listened closely to the explanation. He promised to stay away in a tone which suggested it would not be a problem, that he meant what he said.

'What is it?' his father asked, when he had finished giving his directives.

Kit Siang shook his head. 'Nothing.'

Ah Pak crossed his arms and waited. They could hear the animated conversation going on outside the closed doors, and he knew that politeness demanded they soon join everyone.

'It's just been a difficult time,' Kit Siang began, picking his words carefully. 'I know how much trouble I caused, I've been thinking about it a lot.' Ah Pak was amazed, but said nothing. 'I feel so bad about it.'

He fell silent, picking at the knees of his pants. 'It's about time I settled down, got married. You know.' He paused. 'Did they find the person who killed Yusuf?'

Ah Pak shook his head.

Kit Send mumbled something, and Ah Pak strained to hear it.

'Dad,' he began, and Ah Pak began to worry. He never used the diminutive, had always used the formal 'father'. 'Dad, I'm in trouble.'

This is what Ah Pak had feared. 'Gambling again?'

'No, nothing like that. Not now, before. Before I went to Gua Musang. I … I did something wrong,' he began in a rush. 'I fought with Yusuf, and I think I may have …'

'When?' Ah Pak demanded.

Kit Siang hung his head. 'The night he died.'

Ah Pak leaped from his chair and clutched his head. 'No, no, no – don't say it,' he implored his son. 'No. You didn't do anything. You never saw him.'

He began pacing in the small room. 'Kit Siang, did you owe him more money? After I paid?'

Kit Siang, looking even more hangdog, shook his head. 'No, no more. But Yusuf, he kept asking me, he wanted me to come back and gamble again. I know what he wanted, Dad.' That word again. 'He wanted me to lose more money, and I knew I couldn't do it again to you. But you know, he kept asking me. It was hard to say no. He even said he would get me … a woman.'

'A woman!' What had Yusuf been thinking? 'Who?'

'Khatijah,' Kit Siang whispered. 'But I didn't…'

'I should hope not,' Ah Pak shouted. A sudden cessation in the murmur of conversation outside made him calm himself. This was not for the ears of the in-laws.

'Son,' he continued, suddenly intense, 'tell no one about this. Don't talk about it. Don't think about it. You didn't do anything. It didn't happen.' He looked deeply into Kit Siang's eyes as though to bore into them the necessity for silence. 'You're getting married now, starting your whole life. Forget about all of this. It's gone.'

He walked over to the door and opened it, pasting a smile on his face and motioning for Kit Siang to do the same. They walked out to discuss marriage plans in earnest.

Zainuddin had been visited by one of the men from Thailand, though the conversation remained short and unadorned. How could it have been otherwise? Neither was a conversationalist, neither spoke the other's language. Still – and when Maryam heard about it, this was the thing she found most noteworthy – they understood each other. At least, Din understood enough to know he was being threatened and, even more amazingly, decided to take it directly to the police. Osman called her in when Din was ensconced in the interview room at the Jalan Sultan Ibrahim Police Station so she could hear his story for herself.

He sat in the familiar chair, surrounded by the familiar catering offered to their most favoured visitors: iced coffee, curry puffs and cigarettes – the perfect police trifecta. Din had earned such treats as the first person involved in this case to come voluntarily to the police and offer information. He looked up as Maryam entered and instinctively attempted to smooth his hair, which was a mess. She wondered if he ever rose above a state of dishevelment, or inhabited it permanently.

'So, Din, here you are.'

He nodded enthusiastically.

'What happened?'

'These guys came to see me. From Noriah. Collection people. From Patani.'

Maryam considered his telegraphic style. 'What did they say?'

'I'm not so sure.' He finished his curry puff, and looked longingly at another one. 'They spoke Thai. I don't speak Thai,' he explained helpfully, 'so I don't know what they said. But I could tell what they meant, they wanted me to pay up what I owed Yusuf. But Yusuf's dead,' he continued, 'so I can't owe him any money. But I don't want these guys coming back for me.'

'But you still owe …'

He frowned and lowered his head, for all the world, like an angry bull. 'No,' he stubbornly maintained. 'Yusuf is dead.' His look dared her to disagree.

'That's not relevant,' Osman interjected. 'It's still illegal to threaten people, especially over illegal debts.' Din looked smug.

'That's it,' he informed Maryam. 'They can't do that to me. Neither can Noriah. It's illegal.' He paused. 'Anyway, they came to my house, three of them. They don't speak Malay, but I knew what they wanted.'

He turned to Osman. 'I wasn't surprised: I kind of expected it. I knew Noriah would try something.' He shrugged. 'But I don't have it, so what's the point?'

'Yusuf's death was certainly lucky for you,' Maryam said neutrally.

He frowned again, and Maryam realized this was his default expression: brooding, angry and, yes, stupid. She sighed.

'I don't see that,' he said shortly.

'Without Yusuf, you don't think you have any debts. If Yusuf were still with us, would you say the same thing?' She didn't wait for his answer. 'No, you'd have to pay him. But now, all of a sudden, you don't think you do.'

He glared at her, but said nothing.

'So,' she continued, speaking slowly so he might be better able to follow her, 'Yusuf dying was a lucky thing for you. You benefited from it.'

'No.' If he could have pawed the ground, he would have.

She corrected him. 'Of course, you did. How much did you owe him?'

He mumbled something she couldn't decipher, but what did the amount matter? He couldn't pay it whatever it was. 'Where were you the night Yusuf died?'

Din rose from his chair, snorting. 'I came here to report a crime: I'm being ... what's the word for it? Threatened. Yes, these guys are threatening me. The police are supposed to protect me, isn't that right?' He turned to Osman. 'Aren't you? And instead of finding out about them, you're accusing me of other stuff. You have to help me first!'

Osman seemed to take this to heart, and he nodded at Din. 'We'll take care of it. Now tell me again, how did you know who sent these men?

He shrugged elaborately. 'Who else would want to? I don't

owe any money anywhere,' He thought briefly, running through possible debts, but came up with nothing else worth dunning him for. 'Of course, it's Noriah. These guys probably knew Yusuf from when he did business in Tak Bai.'

'Is that where they're from?'

Another shrug. 'I can't really understand them. They speak Thai.'

Osman remembered that. 'Stay here,' he ordered the Bull, as he put his cap on, then straightened it and walked to his car, motioning for Rahman to follow him. Maryam stayed where she was, but did manage to catch the eye of a young officer and order more coffee and cigarettes. Well, nowhere was it written that one could not be at one's ease while investigating a crime!

Noriah's stomach turned as she watched Osman and Rahman alight from the car. She was supervising workmen, as she had been for the last week or so, and she dreaded a scene in front of them which would be reported all over Kota Bharu in a matter of minutes. She stepped towards them in an effort to head them off.

'Sir! What are you doing here?' she warbled, though she had a fairly good idea of what it would be. The Thais were definitely more trouble than they were worth, and they hadn't yet given her a single ringgit, though they ate heartily nevertheless.

Osman surveyed the work before answering. This was apparently going to be quite the destination when completed. 'Very nice,' he told her, smiling. '*Cik* Noriah, I hope you remember me.'

'Of course, I do.' She bridled, her eyes sliding to the men

ostensibly working, but starting to cast interested glances at the police. This talk was bound to cost her money and time, and in order to minimize her losses, she beckoned Osman off to the side, where the workers couldn't hear anything. She stood silently, willing Osman to go away, while maintaining a neutral expression.

'*Cik* Noriah,' he began slowly, as he always did. Rahman leaned in attentively. 'I have heard that there are some men here from Patani, men coming to speak to your husband's customers.'

Her first instinct was to bluster, to deny, to demand an apology and stalk away, but she steeled herself to stand stonily before the police and give away nothing. She concentrated on breathing slowly, and trying to keep herself from turning red. She was somewhat successful.

'You know *Che* Din?'

She nodded, not trusting herself to speak.

'These men visited him. They came to collect his debts to your late husband.'

She tried to look only mildly interested.

'You know gambling is illegal.' She said nothing. 'You can't collect an illegal debt: that's also illegal.' He looked around again. 'What are you building here?'

She cleared her throat. 'A restaurant.'

He smiled and nodded. 'Very nice.' He lit a cigarette and offered her one, but she declined. Rahman accepted gladly.

'So these men from Patani, are they staying with you?'

'Men?' she squeaked. She was unhappily surprised by how high her voice sounded.

Osman nodded.

'I don't know …' She decided to suspend her understanding of standard Malay, and began speaking in the broadest accent she could muster. 'I don't really know what you're talking about … men … from Patani, you say? I can't really understand what you're saying, so I'm just guessing here … so difficult … from Perak, are you? Hmmm … well, I myself don't go to Patani much, it was my late husband. Me, I was just a housewife, I don't really know much about his business, you know how it is … I mean, really … what do I know?'

She was ready to continue, but was gently interrupted by Rahman, speaking with as broad an accent as she was.

'*Mak Cik*, please. Chief Osman is from Perak, true, but I'm from Kota Bharu, and I understand everything you're saying. We're not all *orang luar* (foreigners). Besides,' he seemed almost unhappy to tell her this, 'We've spoken to the Patani police.'

He smiled at her sadly, neglecting to mention how very difficult that conversation had been, with neither side understanding most of what the other said, and yet they managed to ascertain that three men very well known to the Patani police had been hired by a Malay woman from Kelantan whose husband had often come to Thailand to buy whiskey.

The three got drunk before they left (not that rare an occurrence, actually) and told all and sundry in the bar they were being paid good money to go and collect debts, which they had every intention of pocketing. At least one of the bar patrons sought to trade the information for consideration of his own misdemeanors, and the information was passed from Patani to Kota Bharu in the course of an afternoon.

'Naturally,' Rahman continued while Osman watched him, 'we don't want people like that coming to Kota Bharu and threatening our people, or helping people in illegal pursuits. Like collecting gambling debts, you see.' He stood there politely, waiting for Noriah to speak.

And then, suddenly, a divine inspiration came and she saw her way out of the thicket – if she dared take it. And seeing no ready alternative, she did dare. Clearing her throat, squeezing her eyes shut and praying for tears, she adopted the position of a damsel in distress. And if not quite a damsel, then a *Mak Cik* in distress; pretty much the same thing. She opened her eyes with an imploring look on her face and a trembling voice. (She acknowledged this had probably been more effective when she was younger, but, hopefully, she still had *something*.) She put her hand on Osman's arm and looked around her as though threats lurked all around her.

'Din isn't the only one being threatened,' she breathed, her eyes locked on Osman's. 'They've threatened me as well. They came down here, I suppose they knew Yusuf had died and thought that as a woman alone, I'd be an easy victim.' She bit her bottom lip, but thinking that might be too much, she quickly released it.

'They're almost keeping me prisoner,' Osman didn't see how, as she was out here surrounded by men who would be happy to thrash any upstart Thai gangsters if it came to that.

'They're not working for me. No, they're all for themselves, trying to come to Kelantan and prey on us.' Now she actually cried, whether from the pathos of her tale or from real fear she'd be found out and thrown into jail.

'In fact, sir, I was thinking, could it be possible that they came to kill my poor husband just to create such a situation? Thank Din, yes, thank heaven for Din coming to you when I was too afraid to say a word. Such a brave man, so much braver than I ...'

She remained staring at the ground after this extraordinary confession. Would they believe it? Was Din even believable as a brave, upstanding citizen? Osman didn't know him well, so it was possible he would not reject it out of hand. But really, just looking at that unkempt mess might make the police doubt he was anything but the failure he actually was.

Still, Noriah was aware this was her only chance, and she certainly felt no compunction about throwing the Thais to the police. They were odious, and if they hadn't actually killed anyone yet, it was only a lack of opportunity or initiative; they would not be constrained by conscience. In fact, she told herself what she'd just done was a public service and she ought to be congratulated.

Thus buoyed, she looked up at Osman and Rahman, who stood there staring at her, clearly astounded by what they had heard. Well, she had offered them the solution to the case wrapped up with a silver bow, and no one on this side of the border would mourn the incarceration of those three. And it was likely no one in Thailand would either.

Osman could not credit his ears. Just because he wasn't from Kelantan, did she really believe she could tell him this story and he'd believe it? Of course, Rahman was standing next to him and she expected him to swallow it as well, so perhaps it was not a slur on his Perak heritage, but rather a blanket belief that men could be convinced of anything. Even so, casting Din as the hero of the story seemed rather a stretch. He had Din back at the station, and a more unprepossessing specimen would be hard to find.

But Osman had to give credit where credit was due: this account tied up everything, with few loose ends. He'd have the Thais for Yusuf's murder, and he was sure if he mentioned Ruslan's death, Noriah would oblige him by connecting them to that too – as were-tigers if necessary. He could not quite separate his thoughts to offer an intelligent answer to her. He felt like laughing, but smothered the impulse. It would be unseemly in a Perak gentleman.

# Chapter XX

Osman repeated what Noriah had told him to a rapt audience of strong minded women: Maryam, Rubiah and Azrina.

'I'm just not that surprised,' Azrina averred. 'She was so rude when I met her. "Perak?"' She provided perfect mimicry of Noriah's tone and inflection, packing a trunkful of surprise, contempt and distain into those two syllables. 'I thought she was definitely hiding something.'

Maryam and Rubiah remained silent. No doubt the Thais were up to no good, but Noriah's attempt to charge them with crimes they hadn't been considered for was strange.

'Why did Noriah feel she needed to suggest anyone for that?' Maryam asked. 'No one was questioning her about it. Do you think …' here she hesitated, uneasy about articulating such a thing, 'she killed her own husband? Or just that she got carried away with putting the blame on these Patani people?' She turned to Osman again. 'Do you think she planned to tell you this?'

He frowned. 'No, I think she made it up then and there. Maybe she just got carried away with her story, or it came as inspiration to get these guys out of her hair. I've sent some people to pick them up and bring them in, but I'm not sure how much we'll learn from them. At least,' he added philosophically, 'I can send them back to Thailand and get rid of them.'

'What about Din? So brave??'

Osman rolled his eyes. 'It's such a stretch. Anyway, we had to let him go.'

'He's useless,' Maryam interjected. 'Though I think, as far as it went, he was telling the truth: they did come to see him to get the debt from him. Of course, he doesn't have any money, so that didn't work. I imagine they planned to beat him up as an example.'

Even to her own ears, she sounded calm about the prospect, and believed she ought to have been more indignant, but it was hard to get indignant over the Bull, as she thought of Din. 'Do you think he might have killed Yusuf?' Maryam shrugged. 'He certainly benefitted from his death. He insists with Yusuf dead. his debt is erased. Even if it isn't true – and it isn't – it would still be an excellent motive. And he is big and strong; he's capable of killing Yusuf.'

'And stupid,' Rubiah added, completing the catalogue of Din's attributes. 'Don't forget that: it's a major reason why he could have done it.'

Everyone agreed, but was it sufficient?

'How was he when you spoke with him?' Osman asked Maryam.

'Busy eating. It's hard for him to think and eat at the same time.'

Azrina laughed delightedly at this, reassured that detective work was also an art of making wisecracks. Maryam smiled at her.

'He didn't say too much, because he's afraid he'll get tangled up in lies. He's telling the truth about being threatened, though. At least he came to you with that. Whenever I mentioned Yusuf, he just put his head down and glared at me. It wasn't that helpful.'

'And he's a mess. Just look at him,' Rubiah sniffed. 'Really.'

'He's got no alibi for Yusuf's death.' Osman observed.

'What about Ruslan?' Maryam asked, determined to speak normally of the tiger. It would be more suspicious if she kept avoiding the topic.

'Still nothing,' Osman mumbled. 'I just can't accept this were-tiger thing.'

Maryam nodded while Rubiah watched her with frank appraisal. 'Indeed. Why look to the spirit world when it's a real murderer we're looking for? It's just a story.'

She was very proud of herself, feeling as though she'd talked about were-tigers in a disinterested way, even suggesting they didn't exist. Totally rational. 'Could the Thais have done that? It is close to Tak Bai. They could have come and gone and no one would have seen it.'

'And torn out his throat?' Rubiah asked.

'Why not? Killing is killing, you know. What does it matter how they did it if they did do it.'

'That's interesting,' mused Osman. 'I'd never thought of that.'

Maryam looked smug: she'd turned the were-tiger theory on

its head. She was now leading the speculation that no were-tiger existed, looking for a human agency in the crime. But even as she did so, she still treasured meeting her tiger in the night, in her dreams. And by late afternoon, her anticipation would grow, waiting to sleep, waiting to meet the tiger.

# Chapter XXI

Maryam awoke suddenly, with a jerk of her head that left her dizzy. She was not in her bed, or even in her house: even before she opened her eyes, she knew she was outside. The tree she was leaning up against was rough, and a very slight breeze moved around her. She froze, afraid to open her eyes and find out where she was and, maybe, what she'd done. But she feared more the act of standing blind, not knowing her bearings, unable to take charge of the situation and make it right.

When she cautiously opened her eyes, she found she was not too far from home, still in Kampong Penambang, thank God. She was quite near the river, actually, as she looked down. She was already on the muddy part of the bank, leaning against a coconut palm. Another step, possibly two, and she'd have fallen into the water moving at a brisk pace towards the ocean. She swung her head around wildly. How had she gotten here?

Moving cautiously back from the bank, she realized she was barefoot, wearing only an old sarong tied under her arms, as she usually slept. Her hair was falling out of its bun, and to her horror, had small bits of grass and leaves in it. And her hands!

As she lifted them to her head to arrange her hair, she saw them, black with dirt and damp with mud packed under her fingernails. Her feet were also encased in mud past her ankles, and her mouth felt gritty. She was thirsty, and completely terrified.

She looked warily around her, but the *kampong* still slept. The moon was high, it was nowhere near dawn. This was at least to her advantage – she could get back to her home without anyone seeing her. But she couldn't go in like this, she'd have to bathe. It would wake up at least her family, if not all her neighbours, the noise of pails of water being emptied. She crept through the village, ready to run at the slightest noise or glimpse of a passing human, but she was alone in the night, as though covered with a black cloak through which no one could see.

She nearly wept with relief when she entered her own yard, amazed that even the geese made no noise, pretending not to notice her arrival, though their eyes followed her as she walked towards the well. Did they recognize her as another creature, she wondered, as something unnatural?

She went to the well, lifting the full bucket as silently as she could, then stepping in it to muffle any noise. She washed only her hands and feet, unable to take care of the rest until dawn, when the sounds of bathing would cause no comment.

Inside, she shed her sarong and put on another, and tried to pick out at least some of the detritus in her hair, hoping none would land on the pillow as witness to … whatever this was. Cautiously, she slid into bed next to Mamat, closing her eyes to look asleep should he wake.

'Where have you been?'

She nearly jumped out of her skin hearing Mamat's voice, low but angry.

'I was outside,' she answered lamely. 'I woke up near the river.' Tears came to her eyes without warning, and she was overwhelmed with the urge to sob.

'What? What were you doing there? Wait, let me ask the real question: what were you doing wandering around at night *kaki ayam* and only a sarong tied under your shoulders. His saying *kaki ayam* , or 'barefoot with chicken feet', especially stung. 'And then,' he began to gather momentum, 'why is your hair full of leaves and I don't know what else? And you've washed, I could hear it, but why?' He grabbed her hand and switched on the light, and now Maryam could see the extent of the dirt, visible under her nails and in every crevice of her skin. She began to cry.

'Don't, Maryam,' Mamat continued. 'Crying isn't going to change anything. What's happened to you?' He pulled her hand roughly. 'I'm not even thinking you went out to meet another man, coming back here filthy, like an animal. No man would want that ...'

His voice petered to a stop, and he looked at her more closely, a growing horror in his eyes. 'You're a *hala*,' he said flatly, abruptly releasing her hand and standing up. 'It's happened.' He turned away from her. 'Go down and wash yourself,' he ordered. 'There's no need to hide anything anymore.'

Maryam miserably stood shivering before her well in the middle of the night. Again, the geese watched her carefully but made no noise, and Mamat sat out on the front porch, smoking cigarette after cigarette without stopping. She brushed her nails and hands until they bled and scrubbed her feet raw. She brushed her hair and washed it, wrapping it neatly on her head as she always wore it. She changed into day clothes, sure there would be no more sleep gotten tonight. Thus humanized, she made coffee, bringing cups out to the front porch where Mamat stared straight ahead, not acknowledging her.

'There's coffee,' she said unnecessarily. He could see it. He could hear it if he chose to. He did not.

Maryam took her coffee and sat quietly at the top of the stairs. Things certainly looked different in the middle of the night. She'd never sat out here at night to see it. Of course, why would she? This was the time of night when people slept and rested for work the next day. They did not have coffee in the middle of the night to explain why or why not they were were-tigers. She started to cry again.

'Mamat,' she sobbed. 'Help me.'

He didn't turn his head. 'I don't think I can,' he said with little expression. 'This is beyond me. You chose this, didn't you? You're following the tiger, you can't let it go. I know how you are, but I didn't think you'd choose a tiger over all of us.' He tapped his cigarette unnecessarily hard against the railing, nearly breaking it.

'Didn't everyone tell you to stop it? Didn't Pak Lah tell you not to follow a *hala*? Everyone told you, but you wouldn't listen. I never believed it would get this far.' He turned to her, frowning. 'Did you find any blood? Did you kill anything?' he demanded.

'That would be the end, Maryam. If one of our neighbours comes here with a dead goat, or a half-eaten chicken, I don't know what will happen to you. I really don't.'

'Why can't you help me?'

'Because,' Mamat was now really angry, 'No one can help you if you choose this path. You have to turn away from it. I can't drag you away.' He lowered his voice, realizing how silent the *kampong* was. 'You have to tell the *hala* not to see you anymore,' he hissed. 'I can't. Pak Lah can't. It will know if you're just saying it or whether you truly mean it. Is this the life you want? Tell me.'

'No,' she sobbed. 'I don't want to be a *hala*.'

Mamat made a disbelieving noise but said nothing. He lit another cigarette and kept his eyes away from her. She had never felt so alone.

'Do you even know what you did tonight while you were out?'

She shook her head dumbly.

'No idea? So it could have been anything. You could have killed someone, and you wouldn't even know. You might even kill our children when you turn.'

Maryam was suddenly colder than she had ever been, and fought the urge to check on her children. Mamat looked at her knowingly.

'You can't stay here anymore,' he said, almost sadly. ''Until you really leave it behind, I can't put us all at risk. After all, you might do anything during the night. Would you even recognize your own children?' He sighed deeply.

'Maryam,' he said, and until tonight he'd never used her full name like that, as though he was now distancing himself from her. Which, indeed, he was. 'For God's sake, choose one life or the other. I never thought I'd say anything like this to you. Never! But I'm saying it now. Choose a path, or it will choose you. If you don't really choose your human life, you'll be a *hala*. Maybe you already are.'

He walked into the living room and closed the door.

# Chapter XXII

It was all over Kampong Penambang, and probably all over the *pasar besar*, the main market, as well. Rubiah took charge, sending her husband Abdullah and her two daughters still living at home to stay at Maryam's house, while Maryam stayed with her. It was now just the two of them there.

Ashikin and Aliza took over Maryam's stall, and Rubiah's daughters took over hers. She prayed she wouldn't lose customers with her girls doing the baking. They were good – after all, she'd taught them herself – but they weren't Rubiah.

Ashikin and Aliza were sick with worry, even more so that their father had expressly forbidden them from seeing their mother, particularly after sundown. He explained she didn't remember anything from her night in the *kampong*, wandering as a tiger, and perhaps, under the spell of the *hala*, would not recognize her own children or grandchildren. Therefore, they had to take all possible precautions.

Her daughters could not bear thinking about it, and no one knew what exactly Yi thought, but he looked paler than usual and slept with Mamat rather than alone in his own room. Rubiah turned the day upside down, insisting they remain awake from evening *maghrib* to *subuh*, leaving Maryam no time to turn into a tiger while she was asleep. It gave everything they did an unreal feeling, as though they were already living the life of spirits, isolated from the human world. Just when the *kampong* blossomed into life, they went to sleep, and all night, when decent people were sleeping, they were awake, talking to God and each other. And though they talked through much of the night, they spent much time in prayer, beseeching God to bring Maryam fully back to human life, and free her from the thrall of the spirit world.

Rubiah schooled herself not to berate Maryam for following the *hala*, or even being attracted to it somehow, but she was not always successful. There were times when her anger overcame her, for Maryam had deliberately courted the were-tiger, she'd followed him when all around her advised against it, and everyone, including Maryam, knew what the end would be. There was no flirting with *jinn*: you ignored them or you married them.

Maryam was mortified. Everyone knew she had turned into a tiger, though she herself was not so sure; strangely enough, given her situation, she wasn't sure were-tigers were real at all, or that her own experience was not simply temporary madness. Rubiah tended to agree it was possible, but nevertheless treated the worst possibility while hoping the actual cause was something more benign.

Maryam tried mightily to explain to Rubiah what had happened to her that one night, and why she was roaming the *kampong*, but in the end she could not, as it was a mystery even to her. Deep in prayer, she would search for a memory of that night, how her hands had gotten so covered with mud, but her mind remained a resolute blank and she recalled nothing. That frightened her most of all, for if you remember nothing, how can you know what you might be capable of doing? Just about anything, she feared.

Pak Lah came by daily to see how she was faring, placing spells and talismans all around Rubiah's house, and on Rubiah and Maryam themselves. Rubiah locked the door and windows in the room Maryam slept in during the day, so she couldn't get out without waking her. It was protection for both of them. And still, through all this, thoughts of the tiger came to her unbidden, and they were not entirely unwelcome.

Osman and Azrina refused to stay away. First and foremost, Osman did not believe Maryam was really a were-tiger: he was not at all sure he even believed there were any. Maryam had been his mentor, his mother, his advisor, and he would not abandon her in trouble. Azrina, too, treasured Maryam's friendship, or mother-ship, whichever it was, and thought of her as her best friend in Kelantan. Azrina did not intimidate easily, and it would no doubt take a full-scale metamorphosis before her very eyes into a large and roaring tiger to convince her Maryam could ever do anything wrong.

Osman tried to stop by after dinner, when he knew they would be awake, and talk to them about the case, which was progressing slowly. Din and Noriah remained the two favourite suspects, and for good order's sake, the Thais were also included here. Osman had been looking for the latter for days, in Kota Bharu and beyond, but had found no trace of them. Noriah professed to be relieved, delighted and grateful that they were gone, and urged Osman to redouble his effort to find them so they could be given their come-uppance, but Noriah's motives were always murky.

Though it made Maryam uncomfortable, she herself believed Ah Pak was also a contender. She was reluctant to bring up his name, since she felt some loyalty to him, and worried that if he were wrongly accused, she would be responsible for it. Kit Siang did not actually occur to anyone, and neither did Puteh, since Maryam considered her a good person and therefore unlikely to kill, unless it was Suleiman, and those were certainly extenuating circumstances.

Suleiman was dismissed by both Maryam and Rubiah as too weak, rabbity and no-account to have actually killed someone, though both would have gained a sneaking respect for him if he had. For now, however, the gumption to actually commit murder seemed lacking in Suleiman, a poor excuse for a man all around. And since Maryam now decided she liked Khatijah, who she now believed had strength of character, she dismissed her as a suspect out of hand. Rubiah did not.

As Ashikin's time neared, Maryam felt her helplessness ever more keenly. Now of all times, she should be with her children, and Ashikin in particular, helping her through the birth and taking care of Nuraini and Daud so she could rest. And instead of helping as a mother should, she was imprisoned as a tiger and a threat to the baby. Maryam had never been so despairing.

And then the evening arrived with Osman looking particularly grim and almost frightened. (And as long as she had known Osman, the only things she'd ever seen really frighten him were his mother and speaking Kelantanese.) He stood on the stairs leading to Rubiah's porch, turning his hat around in his hands, close to tears.

'*Mak Cik*, something's happened.'

'What is it, Man?' she asked with concern.

'We found one of the Thais on the road to Tak Bai.' Maryam stayed quiet; there was clearly more to come. 'He's … he's dead. Just like Ruslan.' He gulped. 'It looks like a tiger killed him.'

'Where are the others?'

Osman shrugged his shoulders. 'I don't know. We're calling the police in Patani again tomorrow, to see if they came home. If they haven't yet, they will once they find out what's happened. It's near the place we found Ruslan.' This in particular seemed to make him unhappy. 'I think there's a tiger there,' he whispered. 'I think it's killing these people.'

'A real tiger? A man eater?'

'No. I don't think it's that. No animals have been hurt, and a tiger would go for livestock first. This is a *hala*, and it knows what it's after.'

He sat down on the step, ashen. 'Why is this happening to me?' he blurted. 'I've got bodies everywhere.'

'Don't get dramatic,' Maryam ordered him. 'You're the chief of police. If you fall apart, what will other people do? If you become frightened, what will happen to everyone else? There will be chaos here, *Che* Osman. You have to show us your courage and your wisdom, so we can follow it.'

She was proud of her speech, even though she herself certainly did not look to Osman for courage and fortitude, but perhaps it would stiffen his spine to think so. He did look somewhat surprised to hear he was a leader of men in Kota Bharu and that he set an example for calm in the face of danger. But if so, now would be the time to live up to that image.

He shook his head, however, unable to measure up to the ideal just yet. '*Mak Cik*,' he bleated, 'I think this is a real *hala*. Before I thought it was someone who wanted to make it seem like a tiger, but now ...'

'Why couldn't it be someone really wanting to make it look like a tiger? If they killed one person like that, why not two?' Maryam asked, somehow feeling heartened. She wasn't a *hala* either! Of course, there was the problem of wandering around the *kampong* at night on all fours in the mud. However, perhaps there was another reason for that, even though she was at a loss to identify it at the moment.

Osman regarded her miserably. 'Why do it twice?'

'Why not? Rubiah!' she called, 'Come here, please! I want you to hear this.'

Rubiah bustled in with refreshments, set them down in front of Osman, but not too far from Maryam either, and then registered the look on Osman's face.

'What happened?'

'There's been another tiger killing,' Maryam informed her

happily.

It was, indeed, unseemly for the news to cheer her as it had: after all, someone had died, even though that someone was a gangster and would probably not be greatly missed. But Maryam's mood soared with the news: someone had been killed by a tiger and it wasn't her, she had nothing to do with it, and the second killing convinced Maryam there was no were-tiger, but simply a guilty human. In fact, she was as convinced of that as Osman seemed convinced now there was a *hala* on the loose.

'Where?' Rubiah asked, with some trepidation.

'In the same place as Ruslan died, up near Pengkalan Kubur. And,' she added, knowing Rubiah was thinking the same thing, 'it wasn't me.'

'Of course not!' Osman was scandalized, but Rubiah only nodded, listening for the rest of the story.

'Tell her,' Maryam urged Osman.

'They found his body at the same part of the road between Tumpat and Pengkalan Kubur,' he began, 'and it was the same thing, the throat torn out and the blood all gone. But this time, the body hadn't been dragged to the forest in the back – it was left right next to the road so anyone passing would see it. He was all crumpled up, looking frightened. The police from Tumpat were there again, and I could see they thought it was a *hala*.'

'That doesn't make it true,' Maryam interjected.

'I know,' Osman agreed glumly. 'But they still looked at me like it was my fault for not believing them in the first place. The Tumpat Police Chief said maybe I didn't really understand

Kelantan.'

'Ah, so that's what you're so upset about.'

'No,' he whined. 'It's just that I feel like …'

'This has nothing to do with knowing Kelantan,' Rubiah said briskly. 'Don't let these people push you around.' If anyone was going to push Osman around, it was the two women in front of him now, and they had no intentions of allowing anyone else to invade their territory.

'They think you'll be *mabok tahi telinga,* dazed by talk in your ear, and then you'll listen to them. But you're the chief here, not someone from Tumpat! Though I don't have anything against them,' she cautioned, 'I don't like them treating you like this.'

'It isn't that …'

'What is it then?' Maryam looked up from the cake assortment she was studying with new-found enthusiasm. Her mood lifted higher every moment, and with it, her appetite.

'I think I didn't take them seriously enough when we found Ruslan. I ignored them talking about a *hala*, I didn't want to hear it.'

'And you were right,' Maryam congratulated him. 'Otherwise you'd be off pursuing some nonsense. That was good thinking.'

'Was it? I don't know.'

'Stop it. You were right, this is a person – not a tiger, not a *hala*.' With that, Maryam announced to the world she was back.

'And we must find him before he kills again.'

# Chapter XXIII

She was walking stealthily through the *kampong*: silently, gracefully, menacing. She heard everything, even the faintest sounds: mice scrabbling under the ground, the river moving towards the ocean, even the faint snoring of people asleep in their houses. The variety of smells and their intensity almost overwhelmed her: she'd never experienced smells so viscerally before. Her night vision was extraordinary. Nothing, no one, could escape her should she choose to pursue it as prey. She was the smartest, most powerful being in the village, and the most alive.

She walked close to the ground, with her immensely powerful shoulders down, her whole body nothing but muscle. Strong as she was, she had exquisite control over every inch of her, and it would be nearly impossible for her to make a clumsy move, or even an uncontrolled one. She was immeasurably steadier on her four feet, with large paws which gripped the earth, and able to jump higher and faster than any other animal. She was a tiger, and all her senses, all her perceptions, were unbearably sharp.

She walked down the path admiring the *kampong* as she

had never seen it before. The moon was so bright it seemed like daylight, and her own legs looked so deep a colour of orange, it might well have been part of a different spectrum. The life of a tiger: a heightened, heady existence, so much more real than that of a human being. She could hardly remember what human senses were like, but knew they were of a lower order of magnitude than those she now used, as though she had lived her human life smothered under a blanket, unable to really see, hear or smell. And movement! When as a human had she ever moved with such authority, such swagger, such beauty? She did not believe she could ever revert to her old existence, she would have to follow her new self, her enhanced self – her tiger self.

She awoke with a start, staring uncomprehendingly at the darkened porch on which she sat. She looked at herself, bewildered: she was a person, a *Mak Cik* in an everyday batik sarong and long blouse, leaning against a house post, cigarette burning in a makeshift ashtray. There was nothing tigerish about her, nor – suddenly – were her senses in anyway quicker than they had been. She smoothened back her hair, which needed no adjustment, and picked up her half-smoked cigarette, examining it, unable to credit that her experience had only been as long as it would take to burn halfway down. But she'd been that tiger! She'd felt, she'd known, what it was like to own the night as she patrolled the footpaths.

It was time to call Pak Lah in earnest.

Pak Lah was troubled. He was reluctant to undertake just this kind of action he now believed was the only road opened to him and had spent most of his professional life avoiding. He shook his head sadly.

'*Adik*,' he said to Maryam, who sat numbly in front of him, 'I think there's only one thing to do, and that's send back the *jampi* to the person who sent it to you. I don't like doing it. To me, it's too much like black magic. But in this situation, I can't think of anything else to do. It's clearly a spell, a curse. You're dreaming of your tiger self, but you aren't one.'

'She's right here on the porch!' Rubiah interrupted. 'She didn't go anywhere! That's how I knew …'

'And you're right,' Pak Lah assured her, 'she's under a curse. I can see that now, I'm sure of it. Before I thought maybe you'd chosen it, that you were really turning into a *hala*, but now I think differently.'

'You're sure?' Maryam asked, beseeching him to reassure her.

He nodded. 'I am. Now we know what we're fighting. And I will fight it,' he averred, metaphorically rolling up his sleeves. 'I want you to stay here for a few days, to keep up your strength. But I also want you to take heart, because you aren't a were-tiger.'

Pak Lah rose, still frowning slightly. 'We'll start tonight,' he announced. 'I'll tell your family.'

Puteh could no longer keep herself away from Khatijah. She had wanted to see her before, but was reluctant to face her, believing it had to be Khatijah's fault Suleiman divorced her, since he was too weak and … well, passive, to do it himself. She'd heard Khatijah had returned to her parents' home in Kampong Tikat and, leaving her two eldest to care for the five youngest, Puteh set out on foot for the village at the bend in the road.

It was hot, walking during the day, and by the time Puteh found the house, she already looked exhausted: the hair around her face was wet, her feet were dusty and her cheeks were red. Khatijah took one look at her from the porch of her house and urgently called her up onto the porch and blessed shade.

'*Alamak*, *Cik* Puteh, look at you! You must be exhausted, walking so far in this heat!' She bustled around her, setting a pillow in front of the wall, grabbing a paper fan and calling a young cousin over to buy some cold drinks and cakes at the stall on the road.

She looked at Puteh with concern. Her cousin brought out a small towel soaked in cold water so Puteh could freshen up, and offered a large bottle of Green Spot orange soda as cold as the stall could get it. Puteh was inordinately grateful for the attention.

'I knew it was you,' Khatijah told her, fussing around the porch, 'and I'm very happy you're here, of course. But why come during the day?'

No one had fussed this much about Puteh in recent memory, and she enjoyed it. A small girl toddled on to the porch and grabbed Khatijah's sarong.

'*Intan!*' Khatijah scooped her up and nuzzled her face. 'Siti Hawa,' she said proudly to Puteh, 'my daughter.'

Puteh made all the right noises of congratulation and admiration, but really, she had seven kids at home and how enthusiastic could she really be about one more? She recognized how entranced Khatijah was with her daughter, and maybe she'd also been that way about her first, but she couldn't remember anymore. Khatijah had very graciously got her out of the sun and deserved at least that much from her. They smiled at each other and Khatijah sat down with Siti Hawa on her lap.

Khatijah began. 'I'm very glad to see you, *Cik* Puteh, as I wanted to apologize to you. I was wrong to marry your husband, I know it, and maybe I even knew it then. We weren't married for very long, but it must have made you very unhappy, and I'm sorry. I hope you will forgive me.' Khatijah leaned back with a serious face and watched Puteh, who struggled with an appropriate reaction.

What could she say? She didn't want to forgive her: she had come to berate her, maybe even drive her to tears. But Khatijah had been so decent to her, caring for her even for the few moments when she arrived, and then apologizing. It completely took the wind out of her ire, yet she would hate to leave having said nothing except 'never mind'.

'*Cik* Khatijah,' she began slowly, keeping her eyes off Khatijah's face, 'I came here to scold you, and you have been so nice to me it's hard for me to do so. But I feel I must, even so.'

She took a deep breath. It had never been natural for Puteh to stand up for herself, and it wasn't getting any easier.

'You knew what Suleiman was. He's weak, and you can lead him around very easily. He doesn't think for himself much. He never did. That's his fault, I know. But you knew he had a wife and lots of kids, and if you had not suggested marriage, or didn't look like you wanted it, he'd never have the energy to do anything like that. And because I know him and the way he is, I'm blaming you for what happened, because only you could have started it.'

She leaned back against the wall and finally lifted her eyes to Khatijah's face. Khatijah blanched, and continued to lose colour in her face. Her voice, when she answered, was rougher than it had been, though still well under control.

'I agree with you, *Cik* Puteh,' she began. 'I know that is something Suleiman would never would have done on his own. Well, you can't get married on your own anyway, but that isn't what I mean. I agree: he's weak and he's passive, and it was my fault we got married because if I hadn't moved things forward, he'd still be sitting at a bar mooning after me like a buffalo calf. So you're right, there.

'But *Cik* Puteh, it can't be all my fault. I mean, another woman might see him staring at her and then talk to him, and if she wants to get married, you know he'll do it all over again. But I realized right away that this wouldn't work, so I told him to go back to his family. What will you do if someone else doesn't tell him that, if they hang on to him. Then what?'

They were both quiet for a moment, then Khatijah continued with escalating fervour. 'Will you blame everyone else, or finally blame Suleiman for being weak? He is the father of your children, but I was the one who told him to go back to them. You can't always depend on other women to watch out for your interests with your husband. So, I would say you must control him if you can, and I really think you should. It's very … dangerous, otherwise.'

She leaned back against the wall of the house, her own cheeks now very pink and her eyes narrowed. Siti Hawa didn't know anything of what was transpiring in front of her, but felt instinctively that things were awry and began crying. Her mother made comforting noises and stroked her head. She said nothing to Puteh, but shot her a look that clearly said that this was indeed her fault, and she should be sorry for it.

Puteh sighed loudly. Here she had come to berate Khatijah, and now she was feeling guilty for making the child cry. Why was everything her fault? But in her heart, she knew where the real culprit hid, and that was the useless Suleiman, who created misery around him wherever he went. She tried one more time. 'Why are we two arguing, *Cik* Khatijah, when it's really Suleiman's fault? Yet he sits happily at home at we glare daggers at each other.'

Khatijah said nothing, but watched her with compassion over her daughter's head. Puteh was stuck, that much she knew; with seven kids and no money, where could she go? Khatijah thanked heaven she didn't need Suleiman – indeed, didn't need any man, including Yusuf, so as to be a hostage to what they wanted.

She tried to think of a way to free Puteh from the trap her marriage had become, but every thought she had on this subject seemed to end in a wall, and she could think of nothing helpful. It was disappointing, for Khatijah prided herself on her ability to see her way out of situations other people might take for hopeless. But in Puteh's case, there might really be no way out.

In Kota Bharu itself, around the same time, Munira decided it was time to leave her house and the life she lived and escape. She planned to flee to her sister's house in Pasir Puteh, down the coast towards Trengganu, and never return to Kota Bharu and the hand-to-mouth existence she'd led since getting married to Ruslan. They'd both seen his end approaching, and neither could think of any way to avoid it. She hadn't imagined such a painful and bloody death for him, true, but she knew his life was drawing to a close and he had essentially nothing to show for having lived.

Munira could no longer clearly remember how it all went bad so quickly. Thinking of it for no more than a minute at a time, for that was all she could take, she supposed that once Ruslan began gambling, everything began tumbling into that large hole. She remembered herself as a young girl, and quite dispassionately thought of the dreams she'd had for home and children. And certainly Ruslan's family had seen solid enough, with his brother Yunus a paragon of responsibility. Shortly after she was married, however, it became clear that Ruslan was a very different species than his brother, and took no responsibility for anything.

She dreamily thought back on her earlier self and how she had made no effort to curb her young husband, but had gone along with what he wanted, never imagining it would ruin them both so utterly. As she recalled, she had never even really fought it, or fought with Ruslan to change his ways. Instead, she drifted calmly with the current he provided, even pretending that this was a normal way to live. Perhaps it was normal, perhaps everyone calculated their winnings, or more specifically their losings, every night and never planned beyond that.

Her plans for a family, for children, for a life of which she would be proud, all faded without her even acknowledging it. It seemed unbelievable that she had let everything go so thoughtlessly. Perhaps she had believed at some point they would be rescued by parents or siblings. Indeed, they had required constant rescuing, but in the end, their families could not sustain it.

Munira believed Ruslan had welcomed the were-tiger as a way of finally leaving a life he could no longer go on living. No doubt, he had never considered what would become of her, because Ruslan had always worried only about Ruslan, and never anyone else. And perhaps she had also never worried about anyone at all, not even herself. Even now, she could not achieve histrionics or simple tears, but only look calmly, even beyond calmly, at what was happening to her. She wondered whether she should make the trip to Pasir Puteh, or end it right here. She had nothing to look forward to and no reason to believe her sister would be overjoyed to find one more destitute mouth to feed. Though she would do it no doubt – out of familial duty and pity.

Munira sat on her small and ragged pile of belongings and stared vacantly into the street.

She would have to do something, but she didn't know yet whether she'd have to do it *now*.

# Chapter XXIV

The search for the other Thai thugs had yielded nothing. Osman could find no one who remembered seeing them, and the police in Patani seemed extremely pleased to report that none of them had returned home. Upon further urgent questioning, they admitted they were perfectly happy to maintain this state of affairs, and not at all anxious to remedy it by looking for them. In broken English, the police chief informed Osman they considered it a gift and, indeed, hoped never to find them again in their district. In fact, Osman was welcome to the hoods if he could ever catch them.

He hung up the phone, which had been a real trial, between static on the line and imperfect English on both sides. He was surprised he actually understood anything, but the gist was clear even if the words were not: Thailand had just gladly washed its hands of these men, and no further phone calls would change it. He felt abandoned but didn't know why, since they hadn't been working together anyway. It was up to Malaysia now.

Accordingly, he had Noriah brought into the station, as he himself was too listless to go out to her house and track her down.

Maybe the atmosphere here on Jalan Sultan Ibrahim would impress upon her how serious this really was and encourage her to finally cooperate. She was brought in looking put-out and unhappy, her former wide-eyed entreaty now morphed into flintier irritation.

'Why are you bringing me here?' she huffed as she sat down in the interrogation room, allowing her opinion of the décor to show on her face. 'You know I'm busy, what with the building and – '

'Did you know one of your Thais was found dead near Pengkalan Kubur?'

'My Thais? I have no Thais.' She leaned back with her handbag on her lap, ready to leave immediately if possible.

'You're not answering me.'

'I didn't know any of them were dead. How would I? I haven't seen them.'

Osman's patience was quickly evaporating. '*Cik* Noriah,' he began, gritting his teeth, 'we have two men who've been horribly mauled near Pengkalan Kubur.'

He then recalled Maryam's advice regarding the evidence. 'It looks like a tiger, but we don't think it is. We think it's a person trying to make it look like that. I don't know why either of them was killed, but I can tell you I know both had a connection to you, and I think that's significant.'

He wished Maryam were here. She'd know how to talk to this *Mak Cik*. But Maryam was still in quarantine and Rubiah would not leave her, so he and Rahman were on their own. He felt lost as he steeled himself for the answer.

Noriah considered her options. 'These Thais you talk about, why do you think they'd be connected to me? You've told me that before, but I told you, they just came down here to prey on me, not because I hired them. Or anything.' She was stopped by the look on Osman's face.

'We spoke to the police in Patani,' he said tiredly. 'Your men were bragging in some bar about being hired to come here. I can't wait any longer for you to finally start telling me the truth.'

Noriah sat silent.

'*Mak Cik*, you will be our guest tonight,' he told her politely. 'Maybe after that, you'll start cooperating.

'I don't know,' he said to Rahman, suddenly feeling too tired to even move his legs. 'I can't stay polite when all around me, I see people trying to deceive me. It can only mean they're hiding something awful.' He sighed, and Rahman looked sympathetic. Noriah looked alarmed.

'Look,' she instructed him, 'I think you may have misunderstood. I mean, just not understood my Kelantanese, and so you've drawn – '

Osman shook his head. 'No.' he said curtly, and turned to leave.

'You know,' Noriah began, tripping over her own words, 'I don't think I should be staying here. I'm not a criminal, you know.'

'That's just it,' said Osman, smacking the doorjamb for emphasis. 'I don't know. And you can stay here until I find out. I'm just so tired of this.'

With that, he closed the door and left for home. He was more exhausted than the day really warranted, and he attributed it to listening to lies all day. His head pounded, and by the time he reached his house, after the shortest of walks, he was already pale and feverish, alternately hot and cold. Azrina took one look at him and hustled him directly into bed, immediately administering Panadol and hot tea, and he had never been as grateful for her presence as he was just then.

Noriah, meanwhile, was escorted to her cell, where she was dumbfounded by the accommodations. She sat alone, wondering how she had come to this, locked in a dirty jail cell of all places. Surely this was all a terrible mistake, and she'd be released momentarily with sincere apologies and be driven home where she could clean up and relax. She couldn't do it here, it wasn't possible, and anyway, where was that young policeman who was no doubt on his way to take her home and grovel for the mistake? She smoothed her sarong and closed her eyes, imagining herself elsewhere, refusing to think about the death of that Thai and where the other two might be. It didn't matter to her anyway, as long as they were out of her house and life.

Perhaps, she thought pragmatically, it was just as well he was dead, unable to contradict her story. She would not like the police having long discussions with them – if that were even possible, given the language barrier.

She began to feel forgotten here in this awful place and called out to Rahman, whose name she couldn't remember. 'Young man!'

Rahman knew she meant him. He trudged into the cells, dreading the discussion.

'Young man!'

'*Che* Rahman.'

'Yes, *Che* Rahman. I know you realize there's been a terrible mistake and I shouldn't be here.'

Rahman stood quietly, not wishing to be rude to a *Mak Cik*.

'I didn't do anything, and I certainly don't know those men, so what could I tell you?'

'*Mak Cik*, it's no use in saying that anymore. They already told us. The police in Patani, I mean, and we know you hired those men. It would be helpful ...' here he hesitated, knowing it was a doomed request, 'if you would just stop denying what we already know.'

To his amazement, and it would have been to the amazement of everyone who knew her had they witnessed it, Noriah began to cry. Silently, without sobbing, with tears running down her face. It alarmed Rahman, who wasn't sure of the correct etiquette when a *Mak Cik* cries, because he had never seen it. He rushed out for a box of tissues, which he thrust at her and then backed away.

Looking at the ground, not raising her eyes, she told him, 'I can't stay here, I really can't. I've got to leave.'

On this point, Rahman was clear. 'I'm sorry, *Mak Cik*, you can't leave. We need the whole truth.' He almost smiled, sure that Osman would be proud of him.

'It's just that ... I'm not the kind of person who should be here,' she sniffed, looking woebegone.

Rahman worked up his courage, threw back his shoulders and acted as a real policeman, not a well brought-up *kampong* boy, would act.

'*Mak Cik*, there is no kind of person who should be here, unless they've been involved in a crime. And I'm sorry to say, that's you, *Mak Cik*. And you've been lying since you started speaking to us. Maybe if you stay here overnight, it will give you a taste of what it will be like if you really end up in jail, for years instead of one day. You won't like that either, but believe me when I tell you, *Mak Cik*, that is what you're looking at.'

He walked out of the cell area and back to his desk. He was sweating, and his hands were shaking. What if his mother and grandmother had heard him talking that way to a woman her age? Old as he was, they'd twist his ear until he screamed.

The next morning, Osman was in bed with a fever, brought on by his frustration with the case and an almost universal lack of cooperation on the part of any of his suspects. His yearning for some clarity was almost physical, a longing so intense it couldn't be ignored without causing harm.

Azrina was sure this had made him ill and continued to sap his strength. She forbade him to think about the case, but he tossed in a feverish half-sleep dreaming of tigers and jerking himself awake, disoriented and a bit frightened.

Secretly, Azrina cursed the case. It was all this talk of were-tigers that had invaded both Maryam's and Osman's minds, leaving them weak, confused and defenseless against any malevolent forces which might choose to attack them. And the killings seemed to have unleashed no end of these forces, which threatened to fell anyone connected to it.

But she was determined it would not vanquish her, and she would not allow it to bedevil her husband. She would call a *bomoh* and start her counterattack.

Noriah was much the worse for wear after her night in the cell. She had not slept, but waited all night for Rahman to realize his mistake and come to take her home. He never came, though she pictured him up all night as she had been, tormented by having mistreated a *Mak Cik* and wrongly imprisoning her. But Rahman had long since returned home and gone to sleep without a qualm.

Her involuntary tears of the night before had not led to any confession, or even convinced her a confession was necessary. She regarded it as a nervous reaction to the indignity of jail rather than a sign that she could no longer impede this investigation. If Rahman thought it signaled the melting of her defenses, he was badly mistaken and had not reckoned with the pure steel of her will.

As much as she enjoyed thinking of herself in that way, she was indeed losing determination. A lack of sleep, the horrifying cell, and the threat of remaining there for years to come rattled her badly. Leaning her head despairingly against the bars, she stared at the wall opposite, praying for deliverance.

As did Maryam, though in far more salubrious surroundings. She was comfortable in Rubiah's house, of course, and the food was excellent. Pak Lah began his campaign immediately, sending back the curse on Maryam to the one who sent it.

Pak Lah quietly sat with Maryam and Rubiah, working on getting some essence of the curse from Maryam onto something his *jinn* helpers could use to identify the originator of this spell. He had her lie down and grasp some flowers, while he stroked down her arms with cloths, to drive the *jampi* into her palms and what she held in them, which he would then give to his familiar spirit helpers, his supernatural assistants, his *jinn*. They would then find the culprit and infect them with this sickness.

He was not happy flinging about this kind of malevolence, but it was a horrible thing someone had done to Maryam. Now he believed the best way to cure her would not just be to work on her, but to actively hurl back such evil, thereby freeing an innocent person while punishing the guilty.

Mamat could not sit still, thinking about how he had been so cruel to Maryam when she was the victim of a curse, not the active force in her own downfall. He had blamed her, he had banned her from her own home, when she was the victim. He should have protected her, but had only made it worse, and he was now filled with guilt. He should go to her and apologize, he acknowledged that, but instead, he allowed his own shame to keep him from it. Mamat, plagued by an active conscience, was at every moment planning to see her in an hour or so, but managed to keep postponing it. Still, he realized just the act of seeing her would make him feel better.

Ah Pak was planning a wedding, and should have been happy, but he seemed listless and jumpy. His wife was concerned. Her husband had always been an amiable man, enjoying the groups of men at his store to discuss birds, enjoying his own flock, enjoying his home and family. For the past two weeks, he'd asked his daughters to feed the birds, while previously, he wouldn't let anyone else near them. He looked them over in the evenings with an indifferent eye, not even reaching in to pet them or even bothering to check on whether the girls had actually followed his orders. He was a different man now, an uncaring visitor, shuffling around the house and store with little interest in anything. His wife feared he'd been possessed by a *pelisit* and his soul was in danger. He himself believed he was eaten up with guilt and afflicted by this, and his suffering was really no more than he deserved.

Suleiman was unfocused, but frankly, Puteh could see no difference; he'd always been unfocused. If he moped around the house, what was it to her? She had seven children to take care of, and she refused to allow Suleiman to become the eighth. There were times when she felt she could gladly kill him, and then wondered why she had been so unhappy when he married Khatijah. But it was complicated. Perhaps she had been more insulted that he had gone off with another woman than bereft because she missed him. There was nothing to miss really, an opinion probably shared by most of the people who knew him. As she walked through the house cleaning up, she had to force herself to ask him to move rather than throw large objects at him to accomplish the same thing. Either one would do.

Din was at home, still pondering his options, as he had for several days. He was proud of having gone to the police, and every time he told the story – which was often and loudly – the feat grew larger in his mind, more heroic, more deserving of praise. Hadn't he ignored the danger posed by the Thai gangsters, who surely had no compunctions about killing, and gone to the police instead of staying home, hiding under the *tikar*? He had.

The arrival of the Thais had actually surprised him, as had the assertion that his debt was still owed. He had already decided, unilaterally, that the debt was wiped out by Yusuf's death and would not be dissuaded. No one would get him to pay it, it no longer existed, and if Noriah wanted to pursue it, she'd have to pry it out of him herself.

He could now apply himself to deciding where he might continue to practice his favourite hobby. He leaned toward Tak Bai, since it was in Thailand and there were no neighbours looking disapprovingly at him. He was pleased to have almost come to a decision, and reflected with gratitude on Yusuf's death. Relieved of all debt and obligation, he was now free.

Munira was tired of fighting, tired of living. She had gone to her sister's in Pasir Puteh, actually managing to get herself out of Kota Bharu, but it did no good. She could not see a future for herself anywhere. She had thrown her life away on Ruslan, and not even for love. It was just what happened.

She looked over her pitiful belongings: an extra sarong, a T-shirt, a bottle of shampoo and her *tikar*. It was all she owned now, and would probably be all she'd ever own. She did have a plan of sorts, which she'd been working out in her mind since she had heard Ruslan had been killed.

She left her bundle in the corner – maybe her sister would be able to use something – and walked to the beach. She watched the water for a long time, not even really seeing it, and then, slowly, she walked into the surf, going forward until it was over her head and she could at last feel the tug of the riptide which would carry her far out to sea, where she would never be found.

And Khatijah was fine, home with her daughter and delighted to be there. Yusuf and what he had tried to do to her was a bad dream; Siti Hawa was her reality. She counted herself one of the most contented women in all Kelantan.

# Chapter XXV

With Osman ill, Rahman earnestly attempted to assume the mantle of Kota Bharu police chief (acting), and the first thing he did was go straight to Rubiah's house to plead for her – and Maryam – to abandon their malingering and get back to work. He needed them. Kelantan needed them.

News of Munira's suicide had come in from the Pasir Puteh police, where her sister had gone when she could not be found. Sitting on the steps of Rubiah's house in the afternoon, they were both silent upon hearing the news.

'That poor woman,' Rubiah sighed. 'What a life, poor thing.'

'It's a shame,' Maryam agreed, 'but I think a lot of it was her own fault. You can't just float along, you know. Who knows what Ruslan might have done if she'd taken charge and made him stop gambling?'

Rahman pictured a Ruslan with a wife like Maryam or Rubiah. He'd shape up immediately or find himself back with his parents with nothing but the clothes on his back. Who knew what kind of pillar of the community he might have been if only he'd had the proper encouragement? If he had lived through such encouragement, that is.

'She might have improved his character,' Rubiah continued. 'But we shouldn't talk about him – it's Munira who died. Imagine how unhappy she must have been.'

Maryam was in no mood to wax sentimental about Munira. She was sorry for her, but had little respect for people without the discipline to make something of themselves. 'Yes, very sad,' she said, brusquely dismissing any eulogies. 'I need to ask Pak Lah if I can finally get back to my life.'

Rubiah looked at her carefully: she understood how anxious Maryam was to get back to work on all fronts, but she feared a hidden weakness that might drag her back into the morass from which she'd just escaped. They would see what Pak Lah recommended.

Rahman was dispatched to bring the *bomoh* to the house, and he arrived in the good mood he almost always displayed. 'What's this I hear?' he asked. 'You're wanted back at the police?'

Maryam nodded and tried not to look *too* anxious. After all, she had just recently decreed she was able to enjoy sitting on Rubiah's porch.

'I think it would be alright,' Pak Lah said slowly, his eyes on Rubiah, to see her reaction. She looked calm, which made him all the more confident, for he knew she would have been the most vociferous dissenter if she thought Maryam unready.

'I think you can go home.' He smiled, 'I'll bring some *jampi* to your house later.'

'Can I see Ashikin?' she asked.

'If you're cured, you're cured,' he told her. 'I wouldn't say so if I didn't think you could do everything you did before.'

'I must see my children first,' she told Rahman as she stood up, stretching in the open air as she had not been able to for such a long time. She fairly hopped down the steps on her way to her house, where she was greeted this time with enthusiasm by the geese who guarded the house. She looked at them, and they returned the look, edgily, as geese do, but clearly recognizing her as the human who owned the house.

This bedlam brought Aliza to the door, and she flung herself into her mother's arms. 'I missed you,' she mumbled into her shoulder, beginning to cry from relief. 'I was afraid you were never coming back.'

'Of course, I came back!' Maryam cried as well, patting Aliza's thick hair. Being away from home had given her new eyes to see her children. Aliza was as tall as she was (admittedly, no great feat) and so pretty, it surprised her. 'You're so beautiful,' she blurted, crying and smiling at the same time. 'I didn't really think about you being so grown up and so …'

Aliza smiled. 'One of Azmi's friends asked him about me,' she whispered. 'Can you believe it?'

'What did Azmi say?' She feared everything had gone to hell in a hand basket while she was gone, but a proposal? She wasn't ready for that!

'No, of course.' She giggled. 'But it was the first time anyone asked.'

'And it won't be the last, *sayang*. It's too early for you, you're still in school.'

She was prevented from immediately diving back into her role as mother by Yi's arrival, which was just as jubilant.

'Ashikin?' she asked. 'Has she …?'

'Not yet,' Aliza informed her. 'Any minute now, I think.'

Maryam feared Ashikin would not want to see her, would turn away from her for abandoning her so close to her time.

'Rosnah is with her, helping. She and Azmi are taking Nuraini.' She paused. 'But you're home now,' she squeezed her mother's arm, 'So Nuraini can stay here.' She beamed at Maryam and even included Yi in the smile, such was the extent of her joy.

'Where's *ayah*?' Maryam asked. She looked around for Mamat, suddenly reluctant to see him and hear what he might say.

'He's at Ashikin's. Let's go!' Not even realizing their mother was reluctant, they dragged her the short distance to her daughter's house, where Mamat sat on the steps holding Nuraini. The child shrieked in delight and held out her hands to her grandmother, while Mamat could not have looked more amazed if he had heard one of the geese begin to speak.

'I'm back. I'm out!' Maryam exclaimed unneccessarily. 'Are you … glad?' She wondered – after it was too late, of course – if it were really a good idea to ask him such a blunt question.

Mamat looked astounded, and then began to blush furiously. Ashikin came to the door, drawn by the voices, and shouted a hello.

'*Mak*! Come up! I can't come down now.' She held her back.

'I think today or maybe tomorrow – I'm so glad you're here to help. Everything is alright, isn't it?' She looked anxiously back and forth between her mother and father. Maryam burst into tears.

Her children swarmed around her, patting her, crying, smiling in their excitement to have her back. In the midst of the bedlam, Mamat stood stock still. The crowd moved upstairs to Ashikin's house, but she lingered on the porch, regarding her father with a frown that usually struck fear into the hearts of anyone around her, but Mamat was oblivious.

'*Ayah*? What's wrong?'

Mamat didn't answer, but continued to stare into the yard. Nuraini had squirmed out of his grasp during the commotion and shrieked with excitement to see her *nenek* again. '*Ayah*, what's wrong?' He waved his arm dismissively, as if to say it was of no importance. Ashikin did not have an overabundance of patience in the best of times, and now she had none.

'Tell me!' she ordered him.

'Nothing,' he mumbled. 'I just hope she's alright.'

Ashikin made a leap of intuition which only she could make, and when she did, it was always with amazing insight.

'You're embarrassed,' she reported briskly. 'You thought she asked for this, that she wanted it somehow. I've thought the same myself, and I was angry too, because I needed her here and she was off being cured of being a were-tiger, of all things!' She snorted with disdain. 'But you know, *Ayah*, she was cursed and we were wrong. Just apologize.'

He said nothing.

'She'll forgive you. Come on in, *Ayah*.' She turned to go in, and saw a figure coming quickly up the path. 'It's Azmi,' she said, squinting into the sun. 'He must have heard she's back. Azmi!' She called to him. '*Mak*'s inside!'

'*Ayah*!' Azmi greeted him with great affection. 'Isn't it wonderful she's back?' He bounded up the stairs to join the others.

Mamat thought about Ashikin's analysis, and agreed; she was right about it all. He should apologize to Maryam, but he was so embarrassed!

Maryam and Rubiah were in the car the next morning, Maryam fairly bouncing with excitement to have her life back. They had been briefed, and knew they needed to get the truth out of Noriah as no one else could. It was *Mak Cik* vs *Mak Cik*, evenly matched.

Rahman had not wanted to interrupt Maryam's homecoming, and he had been plied with so many cakes, he wanted only to go home and sleep – which, in fact, he did immediately upon leaving her house. And now, the next morning, they were all primed and ready to work. Rahman politely left the car to get Maryam, who was blissfully making breakfast for her family, and Aliza came to the porch to ask him to wait.

And then came the thunderbolt.

Rahman was transfixed to the spot. Aliza just stared at him, staring at her. Rubiah could see only Aliza's face, and wondered what had happened to keep her normally bouncy niece so still.

As Maryam walked onto the porch, she could only see Rahman's face: he looked as though he had been hit over the head but hadn't fallen yet. She was concerned, until she walked a few steps and saw Aliza, who was jolted out of her trance by her mother's arrival. With a brilliant smile at Rahman, which fairly staggered him, she wished her mother a wonderful day, hugged her again, and ran into the house, leaving Rahman gaping after her.

Maryam had seen this sort of thing before, when Daud first set eyes on Ashikin, for example, but she hadn't expected it yet with Aliza. Stupid of her, she chided herself – look at the girl! She placed a maternal hand on Rahman's arm and pushed him toward the car. 'She's going to teacher's college next year,' she began conversationally, 'she's a very good student.'

'Perhaps a bit early to be married,' Rubiah added.

'Indeed,' Maryam agreed. 'But maybe not to be engaged while she went to school …'

'True,' said Rubiah. 'Engagement would be alright. With the right boy, of course.'

Rahman's ears, which they could see from the back seat, turned bright red, so red it looked painful.

'She'd want someone who was professional, you know. Army, like her brother, or maybe,' she was suddenly struck with an idea which it seemed had never occurred to her before, 'Police.'

Rahman coughed and attempted to speak.

'Well, we'd have to see if anyone's parents come to see us. Did you know,' she said to Rubiah, her eyes dancing, 'one of Azmi's friends asked him about her?'

'No! Already? Well, she's a nice girl.'

'People say she's pretty,' Maryam said modestly, employing the most common way of praising your children to someone else. 'They say it.'

'And they're right!' Rubiah agreed stoutly.

'Of course, Azmi told his friend "no". I mean she's young, and I guess he didn't think this friend would suit her.'

'There'll be a lot of people asking, you just wait and see. I don't doubt more than one boy will find *nasi dimakan berasa lilin:* the rice he eats tastes like wax.'

Rahman sat woodenly in front of them, hoping Aliza would come out of the house on her way to school, so he could see her again.

'*Bagai punggok merindukan bulan,* like an owl moping for the moon,' Rubiah whispered.

Under ordinary circumstances Rahman would have heard it, as he usually listened intently to their conversation as he drove. But today he was distracted.

Maryam considered they had tortured him sufficiently, and anyway, it was time to see Noriah.

'Rahman,' she barked loudly, and he snapped to attention. This, too, boded well for a prospective son-in-law. Aliza was perfecting her order-giving technique in school, with an eye towards keeping her classroom in line, but it could conceivably work elsewhere.

'Let's go to the station,' she instructed him as she sat back in her seat, grinning. 'I have to get home quickly. I think my daughter's giving birth tonight.'

# Chapter XXVI

Noriah was out of her cell and in the interrogation room: it had been two nights in jail, and she was tired and cranky, in addition to being hungry and irritated. Seeing Maryam and Rubiah did not improve her mood any.

'What are you doing here?' she asked ungraciously. 'And why am I here? Do you know I've been here for two days? Two days! Enough is enough,' she stated with absolute certainty. 'I want to go home now!' She glared at Rahman, who didn't seem to be paying that much attention, certainly not enough to be intimidated by her.

'You look like it's been kind of rough,' Rubiah told her with some degree of sympathy, but not as much as Noriah felt was warranted.

'Rough? How would you like it?'

'Not at all,' Rubiah admitted, 'but then, I didn't hire anyone to come to Kelantan and collect gambling debts either. Really, if you think about that, maybe it isn't so surprising.'

Noriah narrowed her eyes, but thought better of replying. She haughtily accepted the Rothman's cigarette Maryam proffered, and they all lit up as a prelude to getting down to business.

'*Cik* Noriah,' Maryam began, 'we know you hired these Thai men to come and collect gambling debts, so please, let's not waste time arguing what we all know is true. The question as I see it is, did they also kill your husband? Or shall I say, did you hire them to kill him?'

'How can you say that?' Cik Noriah was in high dudgeon. 'Kill my own husband?'

'It's been done before,' Maryam pointed out drily. 'And being loud doesn't make something true.'

*Cik* Noriah was apoplectic. 'I will not be insulted like this, I insist...'

Maryam sighed tiredly. '*Cik* Noriah, I must admit to you that we don't care if you stay in this cell forever. The only way to get out is to answer the questions truthfully, or you'll be getting new clothes to wear here.'

Noriah had taken up enough time, Maryam thought, and had spread enough misdirection. It was her certainty that everyone would believe her lies that annoyed Mariam, and as indirect as Noriah could be, Maryam could be that direct and even more. 'I don't think you'll like it,' she finished mildly. 'But if that's what you want ...'

Noriah's eyes filled with tears, a combination of frustration, anger and lack of sleep. 'I have to go home,' she whined. 'I can't stay here anymore.'

'Of course not,' Rubiah crooned. 'Who would want to stay here? Now, *Kakak*, tell us, what happened with these Thais?' She leaned back in her chair, preparing to hear the story. It would probably be a good one.

Noriah sniffled for a few moments, then took another deep drag on her cigarette. Believing this would be a multiple cigarette story, Maryam came prepared with a whole box of Rothman's taken from Mamat's stash. She placed the box on the table, the better to keep the words flowing. A look to Rahman brought coffee: at least they would be alert. Noriah spent several moments staring at the table, no doubt running through scenarios in her mind to see if any might extract her from the situation, but it seemed nothing looked promising. She began to cry again, out of disappointment this time, and Maryam began to shift her demeanor from magisterial understanding to impatient watch-tapping.

'It was like this,' Noriah finally began, reluctantly. 'After Yusuf died, I knew I would take over the business. Well, it's a good business, you understand, and I want to keep it going.

'But this was my problem,' she held up her hand like a schoolteacher. 'I'm a woman, and how do women collect debts? You asked me yourself,' she nodded at Rubiah, 'and that's the issue. People paid up when Yusuf came to see them because they knew he'd hurt them if they didn't, and he could do that himself. I don't think I could.

'So, what to do? If I can't do it, it doesn't mean I'm just going to let those debts drop. If I did that, I'd have no business very soon.' The other women understood the truth in this, even if they disapproved.

'So, who do I ask? If I get someone from Kelantan to do it, how do I know he won't try to take over the whole thing from me, and then start threatening me? I could get people from Malaysia, but the same problem – especially once they see how much is being made here.

'If my son were old enough,' she said regretfully, 'and I wanted him to go into this business, which I don't, that would be ideal. A family business, you see. But he isn't able to, so I need to find someone who can make people pay, but can't stay here. Then I found some of Yusuf's contacts in Patani, where he bought his whiskey, and had them come down. I thought they'd be in and out, anxious to go home.' She shook her head. 'But they weren't.

'They got here, and God knows what they were talking about. I couldn't understand a word. Well, they're Siamese after all. I gave them the list of people they had to see, and then I thought it was a stupid thing to do, they'd take anything they got away from me.

'I couldn't believe they'd gone to see Din. By that time, I already wanted them out of here. They collected some money, but didn't give any to me!' She threatened to cry again: apparently the memory of this lost revenue was heartbreaking. She took a deep breath.

'I was relieved when Din went to see the police. At last, I thought; the police will send them packing back to Thailand and I'll be free of them. But then no one could find them, and I was worried they'd come after me. I have to say, I was … relieved when the other one was found dead. At least I didn't have to worry about him any more.'

She thought for a moment and then realized how very cold that sounded. 'Well,' she amended hastily, 'then I didn't have to fear him. Coming back, you know.'

She quickly abandoned the attempt to make herself look more concerned about these men. No one would believe it anyway. 'And they won't dare come back here now.' She couldn't keep the satisfaction out of her voice.

'Do you think it was a were-tiger?' Rubiah asked. 'That's what everyone's saying: first Ruslan and then this guy.'

'That's a story to frighten children,' Noriah scoffed. '*They* killed Ruslan. An example, they said, so everyone else would know they meant business when they came to collect.' Maryam was both greatly relieved and stunned to hear it. No tiger. Then who, or what had it been who came to her? She yanked her attention back to Noriah, who was still talking.

Rahman leaned over, fascinated. 'How did they do it? Everyone was talking about it.'

Even though Noriah had just denied any real relationship with them, she looked smug. 'Well, of course, the whole point is to make sure people talk and get the message. I saw what they used: a board with five nails sticking out the bottom at one end. Then you swing it and it tears through whatever you're hitting and shreds it.' Maryam winced just to hear this. 'It looks just like tiger marks. It's a good idea. Clever.'

She looked around at her audience, who did not seem impressed with the ingenuity of it all. 'Yes, it's a vicious thing to do. These Thais; what can I say?'

No wonder Ruslan looked so horrified when he died. To see a heavy board with protruding nails was probably no more comforting than seeing a real tiger. And it must have been so very painful. Poor man.

'You paid them,' Rahman pointed out.

She waved that away. 'I paid them to collect the debts,' she corrected him. 'I didn't tell them how to do it. This was their idea, not mine.'

Rahman did not continue the argument, but was confident a court would not see it that way, and Noriah would get what she deserved.

'So they killed Ruslan, in a particularly frightening way,' Maryam summed up. 'But if it was a warning message, it wasn't very clear.'

Hearing this, Noriah looked perplexed.

'I mean,' Maryam amended, 'everyone heard about it, they weren't talking about anything else. But it was all about the *hala*, not about collecting debt, so it wasn't a message everyone understood.'

'I disagree,' Noriah answered formally, as though they were at a school debate. 'Most people saw it only as a *possible* were-tiger.' She smirked at Maryam, knowing well what had happened to her, and Maryam understood the urge to murder. She restrained herself. 'But the people who needed to understand, they knew. Ask Din. He's not smart, but even he got nervous. I think it worked. Better than if it were, as you say, clearer, since it seemed more …'

'Sinister.'

'Yes, that's it exactly.' Having settled all that, Noriah looked satisfied.

'But they didn't kill Yusuf.' Maryam added, wanting to make sure about it.

Noriah shook her head again and lit another cigarette. Why not? Following her example, everyone else lit their own, finished their coffee, and ordered more, with curry puffs. 'How could they? I only called them after Yusuf was dead, and only because he was dead. Otherwise, he'd collect his own debts, and why would I need them?'

'What about the last body, the Thai who died? That looked like a tiger, too, but there never was any tiger. Was it one of the other ones? A fight over money, perhaps?' Rahman asked slowly.

'I don't know anything about that. Nothing at all.' She shrugged. 'For all I know, it was a real tiger.'

# Chapter XXVII

Her last words both terrified and relieved Maryam, who preferred a real were-tiger to a delusion. She would much rather be in real supernatural danger to being mad. Nevertheless, she had other things to do. She rose from the table: it was time for her to leave and take care of Ashikin. She'd done her job here.

'Wait. Aren't I going with you?' Noriah asked.

'I'll be back soon,' Rahman promised, 'and we'll talk then.'

The prospect of running into Aliza made Rahman blush all the way back to Kampong Penambang and, amazed at his luck, she was waiting for her mother at the bottom of the stairs.

'*Mak*! We need to go straight to Ashikin's. They baby's coming!'

Maryam bustled into the house and emerged moments later with a bag full of things she might need. 'The midwife?' she asked Aliza.

'Already there,' she replied. And as they hurried to Ashikin's, Aliza turned and favoured Rahman with a wide smile, which he returned and then sat down heavily in the car, feeling giddy, and rested his head on the steering wheel.

Ashikin's house was filled with relatives, but Maryam took charge. The midwife said all was going well, and Maryam set about making her daughter comfortable, while the other women cooked. The men waited outside with Nuraini, smoking and talking only fitfully: they were nervous.

Even in labour, Ashikin looked good, and Maryam wondered how she did it. Maryam herself was under no illusions of her own appearance during labour, and would not have wanted any pictures taken to commemorate it, but Ashikin could still carry it off. Looking from her to Aliza, busily wiping her sister's brow with a cold cloth, Maryam marveled at how she'd had such beautiful daughters. Her reverie was interrupted by a sharp poke from the midwife, who told her the baby was just about here. One more tremendous effort, and out he came.

'A boy!'

At his first cry, Daud barreled into the room to see him and assure himself his wife was healthy. He smiled in pure delight. Ashikin, too, was pleased to be finished with the birth and delighted to see her new son.

'Zakaria!' Daud announced, and she smiled in agreement. Daud bent over his son, overcome with tenderness, and whispered the call to prayer in his ear, welcoming him into the world as a Muslim.

As soon as she was cleaned and comfortable, the family rushed in to see the mother and child. Mamat was transported to see his grandson, and he held Nuraini to greet him. 'See: this is your new *adik*,' he told her. 'Now you're a *kakak*, an elder sister, and you'll take care of him.'

Her face clouded. 'No. Why is he here?'

'He's your *adik*,' Mamat repeated patiently, 'and he's just come to meet you. See? How soft his hair is? And he's so little ...'

Nuraini deigned to pat his head softly and smile at him. Then she made it clear she'd had enough and wanted to go outside again and play with Yi, who was more fun than a baby. It promised to be an interesting transition.

Maryam regretted ever having seen the tiger, which had brought her nothing but misery, and wasn't even real. She wondered about it, and whether it was all her imagination as it now seemed it might be. Though Maryam remained painfully aware they still had no idea who had killed the second victim, and perhaps a real tiger was roaming up there. She admitted this was probably more a desire not to admit to herself that she might be completely delusional than any hope a tiger actually prowled the Tumpat district.

And though the most grisly of the mysteries was now solved, they were no closer to finding Yusuf's killer than they had been at the start, though they knew a great deal more about his wife and associates than they had, and the consensus was negative.

Noriah's children had not been to visit her since the first day, and to Maryam, that said it all. Rubiah had asked whether the son would take over the business, and while no one knew for sure, it certainly seemed likely.

It was also likely he would follow in his parents' footsteps in both ruthlessness and strength. As his mother's son, he would surely not let such a profitable business fall, even if he was a bit young to take it over. As his father's child, he made up for his youth in size.

Having at least identified the were-tiger, Maryam and Rubiah believed they were entitled to some well-earned rest, with time to see their families and get to know Zakaria. Neither had said a word to Aliza about Rahman. If he was interested, they'd hear from his parents. And if they didn't, it meant nothing. Any afternoon she was home, Maryam would almost expect to see them attacked by the geese in the yard, but so far, not a sound. Perhaps they misread him – extremely unlikely, they agreed – or his mother had already approached someone else, which was the most likely explanation. Either way, Maryam wasn't particularly anxious to have Aliza married and was sure she would have no lack of suitors. They could comfortably wait to see what developed.

Osman was mending slowly, and Azrina would not allow him to go back to work yet. She was thrilled to hear the were-tiger remained the legend it had always been rather than come to life in front of them, and hoped that this might give her husband some peace. On her own, however, she'd been devising her own theories of what might have happened.

She concentrated on the second killing near Pengkalan Kubur, and who in fact might have carried that out. Wasn't the were-tiger technique overused already? Why do it again when it could be explained? Osman had always told her they were lucky most criminals were not smart, and that's how they got caught. This murder might be the perfect illustration of his point.

Perhaps it was an argument among the gangsters where one killed another one by the same method they'd used on poor Ruslan. And then the other two fled, probably disappearing into Thailand, giving their old hangouts a wide berth so as to remain invisible to the police. From what she understood, the Thai police were utterly disinterested in finding them, so avoiding those 'defenders of public safety' might not be that difficult. As long as they did not become too visible, they were probably safe.

She did not bring up the subject with her husband, who needed time away from this mystery, but could hardly wait to tell Maryam her theory and contribute to the investigation like a real member of the team.

Noriah may have disparaged Perak, but now that her guilt was revealed, her opinions on people from the West Coast were no longer relevant. And Azrina was determined to uphold the honor of her home state and prove that Perak women were just as brave and resourceful as Kelantanese. Of course, this campaign might have been more successful were it launched in Perak itself rather than Kelantan, but she was sure Maryam would applaud the sentiment.

Maryam was concentrating on the crime which triggered all the others. Without Yusuf's death, the trail of mayhem which had consumed Ruslan, Munira, and one of the Thais might never had happened. Yusuf would still be happily terrifying gamblers who couldn't pay, and Noriah wouldn't have any reason to call people in from anywhere to help.

'There are three people who really benefitted from his death,' Maryam explained slowly to Rubiah. She counted them on her fingers. 'Khatijah, because there wouldn't be any pressure from him anymore; Ah Pak, because he wouldn't have to worry about Kit Siang anymore; and Din, because without Yusuf, he thought he wouldn't have to pay.'

She held up her hand as Rubiah began to object. 'I know what you're thinking,' This comment always irritated Rubiah mightily. 'But we're talking about what Din perceived as his benefit, not what was actually true. Now,' she resettled herself on the porch of her house, as Aliza lounged in the door, listening and learning, 'For the moment, I'm going to take Din out of the group ...'

'Because he's stupid,' Rubiah announced, then turned to their eager apprentice. 'You see, Liza, how important stupid can be.'

Maryam turned to notice her, and then turned back to Rubiah. She felt a breakthough coming.

'Right. He is stupid, but also strong and angry, and I could be wrong.' Rubiah felt this to be an entirely disingenuous self-deprecation. Maryam *never* believed she was wrong.

'But I think if it were Din, it would be far more obvious. He'd kill him in broad daylight on the street, and this killing was clever. It was possible the current might have taken the body out to sea, and that would have been an end to it. Unfortunately for the killer, it didn't, but to me it still looks like someone thought it through. Someone a lot smarter than Din.

'And also,' she continued, 'I've been thinking about it, and I don't think it took a lot of strength to kill him. You know what that mud is like by the river: so slippery. So if you could get him off balance, by surprise, you could easily make him fall, and then stick his head into the river before he had a chance to collect himself. It could be done.'

Rubiah nodded. 'Easily, if you planned it, and you knew where he would be.'

Immediately, the two women stared at each other. 'That's who it is,' Maryam whispered.

# Chapter XXVIII

Khatijah did not look repentant. Maryam and Rubiah looked at her critically, seeing her, really seeing her, for the first time. Khatijah was not the small, dark, gnome-like figure Maryam had originally perceived her to be. At first, Maryam had been contemptuous of her, agreeing with Noriah that she was, as they say, *hidup segan, mati tak mahu* – reluctant to live, unwilling to die. Less poetically: aimless and indifferent.

She hadn't married, hadn't had children, worked in a gambling den and, all in all, appeared to have no plan for her life, no interest in taking charge of her own fate. And then when she *finally* met her, and spoke to her for the first time, her opinion spun around, and then she'd admired her. While perhaps revealing a regrettable lack of planning when it came to marriage, and lamentable taste in men, she was in no way a passive recipient of whatever life threw at her. She was an honorable woman, in her way, and a devoted mother.

The steely core of Khatijah's self was now displayed, and Maryam wondered how they had missed it for so long. She now appeared to be determined to do what she needed to protect herself and her daughter, and was not a woman to be crossed.

It was understandable that Yusuf had not noticed that, for Khatijah had always kept it hidden, at least appearing on the surface to drift – an affect at odds with her willingness to act, however ruthlessly, and not look back. She sat now, in the police station, utterly composed, even slightly bored, thinking only of getting back to Siti Hawa at her mother's house.

'Why did you kill him?' Maryam asked.

'Why? I told you why!' Khatijah was amazed, and not a little provoked at the blindness of the question. 'He asked me to become a prostitute! You didn't know Yusuf very well – he was a bully, and he'd never let up once he got something into his head. Even if I quit, it wouldn't have made any difference to him, because he'd never let you out of his grip once you'd gotten into it. I never let him get too close to me, because I'd seen how he was.

'And Noriah's no better,' she advised, 'just more ... diplomatic. They both get their claws into you and won't let go.' She was silent for a moment, and spent the time lighting a cigarette and asking for another cup of tea. 'With milk and sugar,' she reminded the junior policeman, in a quiet and self-assured way. She looked back at Maryam and sighed softly.

'*Mak Cik*, there was only one way for me to get away from them, from the whole thing. The gambling, the serving and, in the end, working for Yusuf as a prostitute. Can you imagine? I wouldn't even be able to keep my own money! He'd take it all. I'd be a slave, or no better than one. Is that a life?'

Maryam had to agree it wasn't, and was actually quite

sympathetic to Khatijah's dilemma. She'd probably have done the same in her shoes, but that didn't matter: it was still murder. She hoped the courts would go easy on Khatijah, or maybe even let her off. The situation she found herself in sounded dire, and who could blame a woman for fighting with all her strength against such a fate? If the decision were left to her, she'd imply tell her to go home and advise her not to do it again. But then, she doubted she ever would do something like that unless the same kind of situation presented itself.

'*Cik* Khatijah, you know you can't kill people just like that,' Rubiah said gently.

Khatijah obviously worked to keep her impatience in check. '*Mak Cik*, please tell me, what would you have advised me to do instead?'

The two adjunct detectives were at a loss. Maryam looked over at the silent Osman, who appeared shamefaced for his lack of a good answer. He knew he could have done nothing to protect her, even if she had called upon him. His involvement would only have made things more dangerous for her, and without a family to protect her against Yusuf and Noriah, a weaker woman might have given in. Khatijah was not, however, the giving-in type. Osman cleared his throat in preparation for speaking, though he had no idea what he might say.

'I tried,' Khatijah explained, 'I got married because I thought it might keep Yusuf away. But Suleiman was useless,' she made a face. 'I pity Puteh, I really do. Poor soul.

'But anyway, it didn't make any difference, and I realized

pretty quickly that wasn't the answer. And, Chief Osman, I needed an answer right away.' She looked at him in frank appeal, with no artifice or drama. He found he liked her and was angry at Suleiman – to have such a decent woman turn to him for help and simply let her down. But then, Suleiman had made a career of that.

'Blame me if you want,' she shrugged. 'I did what I had to. And I've noticed not one of the three of you has been able to come up with something else I might have done instead. Maybe run away to Kuala Lumpur? Leave my home and family and try to live somewhere else, far away?'

No Kelantanese would agree to that, or recommend it to another. Maryam stayed silent.

'No? That's how I felt too. And who mourns for Yusuf?' she argued. 'Noriah? She doesn't. She never did. Suleiman or Din?' She rolled her eyes. 'Please. His children?' She thought for a moment. 'You know, I really don't think so. And that's the saddest part of it all, isn't it?'

She rose from her chair and extinguished her cigarette. 'I've got to go home now. Siti Hawa will be waiting for me.' She addressed Osman directly. 'You know where I am. I'm not going anywhere. If you need me, come and get me. But I really hope you'll think about it, and be merciful.'

She nodded politely at Maryam and Rubiah and walked out the door, to where Rahman waited to drive her home to Kampong Tikat.

Maryam was reluctant to raise her eyes from the table. The

three sat silently, each embarrassed at their lack of alternative courses of action for Khatijah, Osman most of all. He longed to be able to say 'You should have come to me. I would have kept him away from you and sent him off with something he wouldn't soon forget.' But it would be a lie, and surely Khatijah deserved better than that.

'You know,' Rubiah began slowly, her forefinger tracing a design on the table top, 'I understand why she did it. I mean, forcing someone into doing that ...'

'She wasn't forced,' Osman reminded her, though he felt ashamed to correct her. 'Yusuf hadn't done anything to her yet, so she wasn't really forced.'

'She knew it was coming,' Maryam reminded him sharply.

'I know,' he continued doggedly. 'But according to the law, nothing happened yet, so Yusuf wasn't guilty.'

'Of what? Threatening her?' Rubiah looked at him as though she might seriously consider threatening him herself, in order to more clearly illustrate to Osman exactly what she meant.

'Well, threatening yes. But he hadn't done anything ... physical to her.'

'So she should have waited until he beat her? Or locked her up, or forced her to ... you know. By then, it's too late.'

Maryam lit a cigarette briskly and looked at Rubiah. Osman immediately felt outnumbered and outgunned, and knew if Azrina were in the room, she'd be firmly on the side of Maryam and Rubiah. It was depressing, defending Yusuf when he despised him for what he'd done. But the law was clear, and even Khatijah didn't claim she'd been physically coerced. Yet.

'What are you saying, *Mak Cik*?' he asked as he willed himself to breathe slowly and not panic.

Maryam blew a steady stream of smoke at the floor, then looked at him again. 'I'm not really sure, Man,' she admitted. 'I think I'm saying … she was defending herself, the same as she would have been if he held a knife to her throat. And because of that, because she was defending her morals, too,'

Maryam wasn't sure but that she might have gone too far here. After all, this was the woman who married Suleiman: she was no paragon of virtue either. But, she argued with herself, marrying the wrong man and then quickly repenting of it did not constitute an irreparable stain on one's character. It was not a case of *panas se-tahun dihapuskan di hujan sehari* – a year of dry weather ruined by one day of rain – spoiling a good reputation built up over a lifetime by one possibly minor misdeed. After all, marrying the wrong person was practically Kelantan's national pastime.

She squared her shoulders and stopped equivocating. 'You should let her go,' she ordered Osman. 'I know she's killed, but she was defending herself – and that makes it different.'

Rubiah immediately seconded the motion. 'Yes, I agree. That's what you should do.' She began gathering up her purse as if to leave, and why not? Osman had his directive.

'Wait!' he told them. 'Just wait a minute. I can't do that. It's wrong.'

'Wrong? Rubiah asked him, feigning astonishment. 'I'll tell

you what. You talk to *Cik* Azrina about it. And then you can come to the market tomorrow and let's all talk. Maybe your lovely wife can talk sense into you.'

She marched majestically out of the room, and could be heard ordering Rahman to fetch the car. Osman looked up at Maryam for help.

'It's difficult, I know,' she sympathized. 'But sometimes you have to apply the law to do what's fair and what's right. '*Tanak dalam periok*,' that's what we say. Cook rice in a cooking pot: do things the right way. It should be justice too, not just law.'

She was proud of herself for that speech. Who could have thought, years ago, that a *Mak Cik* with a *kain songket* stall would be lecturing the police about justice and law like that. It was very satisfying. Then she, too, drew herself up to full height, picked up her handbag, and walked slowly out of the room.

Rahman already had the car running and the air conditioner blasting, and she slid in next to Rubiah and reported what she had said to Osman.

# Chapter XXIX

Yi stood before his father, clearly uncomfortable, casting longing glances toward the door and the outside, to which he yearned to escape. Manfully, however, he forced himself to do what Aliza had instructed him, more afraid of what she would do to him if he weaseled out of it than of the misery he felt approaching his father on this topic. But he had his orders, as Azmi would say, and he meant to finish his mission or die trying. All three of his older siblings agreed Yi would be the most unthreatening emissary to deliver the message, and Aliza was nominated to make sure he completed his task, and she was not unthreatening at all.

Mamat watched Yi with rising interest, unsure of what he wanted, but ready to give it his full attention. Finally, after much squirming and lip-chewing, Yi squared his thin shoulders, sighed deeply, and began.

'Ayah, we all think ... that is, we all want to tell you that we know ...' Now he began to rush, and speak as quickly as he could to get it over with, 'That you're angry with *Mak* and that you still blame her, but we think you should try to not be angry with her, and to forgive her, and make our family like it was before. We don't want you to get divorced, and people are saying you will, but I hope you won't 'cause I'd be so unhappy if either of you weren't here, and I would be all alone and even Azmi and Ashikin would be unhappy, really unhappy.'

He had done it. Whatever happened now, at least the worst was over, and Aliza could not claim he had failed. He let out a long breath.

Mamat was shocked into silence. The thought of his four children gathering together and planning this, and then dragooning Yi into doing this nearly brought him to tears. They must have chosen Yi because it would be hard for him to dismiss him, as he acknowledged to himself he might have done with the two eldest, and told them shortly it was none of their concern. But with Yi, his baby, he couldn't say that. And he looked up at his father with such questioning eyes, Mamat was ashamed to have done this to him. He reached out a hand and placed it on Yi's shoulder.

'Yi ...' he began, finding, to his surprise, his voice was clogged with tears and he was having trouble speaking, 'Don't worry. I love you all.'

'Even *Mak*?'

He nodded. If he spoke, he would cry. He cleared his throat. 'All of you. I don't want to leave you. Don't worry.' He tried to smile.

'But you never talk to her ...'

'Yi, this will be alright.'

'Not if you don't talk to her,' Yi pleaded. 'Don't you see ...'

'Yi,' he said gently, 'you'll have to leave it to me. But don't worry,' he assured him.

Then he walked slowly into his room so he could cry in private.

Yi was debriefed by his sisters, while Ashikin cared for Zakaria, who was a healthy and already sturdy baby.

'He looks like you,' Ashikin told him. 'His ears stick out.'

'Tell me,' she ordered, while Aliza straightened out the room.

'He started to cry,' Yi reported.

'Cry? *Ayah* cried?' Ashikin asked in amazement. 'I didn't expect that.'

'You must have done a good job,' Aliza complimented him. 'Very moving.'

'And what else did he say?'

'He said he loved us all, even *Mak*, and he wouldn't be leaving.'

'He said that?'

Yi nodded. The sisters conferred. That was good news; at least, he had actually said he wouldn't.

'Did he say he would speak to her again?' Ashikin asked.

'He said he had to do it his way, and that's all he said. There's nothing more to tell. But then he cried, so maybe he'll forgive her.'

'I hope so,' Aliza prayed.

'Me, too. I don't know what I'd do if they separated while I have a newborn. Really, I can't handle everything alone.'

Mamat could not sleep that night, plagued by the memory of Yi taking his courage in his hands to speak to his father about this. His children must have been talking about this non-stop, and it touched him that they'd orchestrated this in an attempt to make things better. As a father, he believed he could not disappoint them, though as a husband, he was still embarrassed and perhaps, he admitted to himself, sulking.

It wasn't Maryam's fault, he knew that now, but it was so hard to make a formal declaration of his mistake. He was hoping that Maryam would apologize to him. For what exactly. he couldn't say, but if she did, he could graciously accept her apology and make things right. Now it seemed he'd have to act first, and it was awkward.

Yet, if he wanted to keep his family together, if he wanted to preserve his marriage, then he had to say he was sorry, difficult as it was for him. He would try. He wasn't sure what to do, but he would force himself to speak with her and not bring it up, and knowing Maryam, she in turn would force herself to be as nice as she could and cater to him for the foreseeable future, which might not be so bad. And she would know, somehow, that his speaking to her again meant he was very sorry for blaming her and would not doubt her again. She would realize that's what he meant when he asked her what was for breakfast and smiled at her, and when she smiled back and said, 'nasi kerabu', that would mean she'd forgiven him and understood how he could make such a huge mistake. He rose from the steps, though it was closer to morning than midnight, and went back into his bedroom.

Noriah was allowed to leave her cell and return to her home, with strict instructions not to leave Kota Bharu. 'We'll find you, *Mak Cik*, if you leave,' Rahman warned, more comfortable with lecturing her now that he thought of her not as a *Mak Cik,* but a criminal – and those were two completely separate and unrelated categories. He watched with satisfaction as she left.

Noriah dragged herself back to her house. Her son came to the police station to bring her back home, but his face remained slack and blank, his greeting perfunctory and without emotion. Though she was hurt by this welcome, she also knew her own greeting was hardly more animated, and wondered dully how they became such an uncaring family, and if they had always been so. She didn't think so, but was no longer sure she remembered anything with accuracy.

She deposited her purse on the living room floor and retreated immediately to her bedroom to peer into her mirror, where she saw an exhausted and disheveled woman, looking far older than when she had left only a few days earlier. Then she was a bustling *Mak Cik*, full of plans and confidence, scheming to avoid the police and primarily concerned with ensuring the construction moved along as quickly as possible.

And now? Was that new gray in her hair? Her clothes were a disgrace after all that time in jail, fit only to be thrown away, the better to forget the entire experience. Her face looked tired and reflected the gray in her hair. She reached up to touch her cheeks, pulling at them anxiously as though she could instill some colour in them. She turned away wearily, trudging down to the well to bathe, wrapped in an even more faded sarong. She hated everything about herself.

Osman slouched home from work that evening, uncomfortable with the afternoon's work and unable to take one side or another. He was anxious to discuss it with Azrina, who he believed had more respect for his intellect than either Maryam or Rubiah. They were of an age to be his mother, he told himself, and therefore would also look on him as somewhat less mature. He shook that off. Now he would talk to his wife.

'I need to talk to you about something. Something at work,' Osman told her at the dinner table. She was all attention.

'This case about Yusuf. It seems we've found the murderer.' Although Azrina quivered with anticipation, it did not pay to hurry Osman. In fact, that would only slow everything down. She sat rigidly, only her nose twitching, but Osman was looking out the window and not at her.

'It was Khatijah,' he said softly. 'She killed him. We never suspected her, but it was her. She swears that Yusuf wanted her to work as a prostitute in the gambling hall, and she said no. She told us Yusuf would never let it go, she knew him, knew she'd never escape him. She claimed this was the only way she could get out of it.' Azrina sat silent.

'*Mak Cik* Maryam wants me to let her go. She says it was self-defense and we shouldn't prosecute her for it. There was a lot said.' He sighed. 'But Yusuf didn't actually *do* anything to her. He just threatened to, you know. So where's the basis

221

for self-defense?'

Azrina gave him a look he had recently come to recognize, a look in which forbearance with his faults was mixed with a wry amusement about just how wrong whatever he had just said could be. Women, he found, seemed to specialize in it, particularly older, confident women, and it was his first inkling that Azrina was a likely candidate for *Mak Cik*-hood, a most promising novice really, who might someday grow into a Maryam. He wasn't sure how he felt about it, but leaned toward relieved.

His wife composed herself in order to deliver her opinion. '*Sayang*,' she began, sugar-coating whatever she planned to say, 'I think you need to look at it from Khatijah's perspective. It isn't just physical threats. I know you know it, but it's, well …

'He did threaten her.' She pursued the logic in a nearly mathematical way. 'He really threatened her life: what kind of a life would she have had if he'd made her do … that. It would be terrible.

'So really, he did threaten her life, and it was self-defense. That's what I think.' She was quiet for a moment.

'It sounds like a horrible family. What kind of a man would try to force someone into that? And Noriah's no better.' And Noriah had also disparaged the great state of Perak, and that irritated more than Azrina cared to admit. Though it was, she acknowledged, childish on her part.

'You can't blame Khatijah for doing whatever she had to do to get out of it. I would do the same,' she said with finality, thereby putting her own stamp of approval on the deed. 'I don't say it's good, I don't say it's … praiseworthy. I just say I think she was fighting for her life, and more important, her daughter's, and it can be self-defense even if he hadn't actually raised a hand to her. Yet,' she added darkly. 'I'm sure it would have come to that.'

Osman considered what she had said, and how the three people he admired most in Kelantan all agreed. If only his mother in Perak had weighed in on Khatijah's behalf, it would constitute a quorum of those he considered wisest.

'I think almost any woman you asked would understand why she did it, whether or not they thought she should be prosecuted. They'd know how helpless she felt.'

Azrina rose and began making coffee to bolster Osman's possibly flagging energy. 'You know, *sayang*, I think you need to temper justice with mercy.'

She wasn't sure where she'd heard that. Perhaps studying for her exams in English Literature. She really liked the way it sounded, and made a note to herself to remember it. It would no doubt come in handy later, when discussing police business.

Osman sat quietly, and Azrina did not interrupt his thoughts. Finally, he approached her again.

'Na,' he began. 'I can't make the decision. Not alone. I'll talk to the prosecutor tomorrow and see what can be done. I'll give him my opinion that it was self defense.' Azrina smiled broadly at him. 'But I'll let him decide.'

# Chapter XXX

Ah Pak walked into the Police Station, his arm tightly around his son's shoulders. Both were pale and a little drawn, and Ah Pak had clearly dressed for the occasion by donning pants, which he wore with his signature undershirt. He asked quietly for Osman when he arrived and propelled Kit Siang into the Chief's office.

Osman smiled and tried to put them at their ease, but they both looked tense and frightened. 'Tell me,' Osman instructed them. 'Whatever it is, it can't be that bad.'

Kit Siang continued to stare at the floor, until prodded by his father. 'I just wanted to tell you … I mean, I want to confess.'

Osman sat quietly, if somewhat confused.

Kit Siang gulped. 'I had gambled in Yusuf's place,' he began his preamble. 'I lost a lot. My father asked me not to, but …' Kit Siang seemed at a loss to explain it in more detail, but Osman immediately understood.

'So when I lost the first time, it was big, and he went to talk to my father. He told me it would be alright, my father would never let anything happen to me. I was so stupid,' he moaned. 'I never even thought about what he meant by that, even though I knew how he collected gambling debts. The other guys talked about it sometimes.

'Then he asked me to come back. "You'll be luckier this time," he told me, but, of course, I wasn't. The loss was even bigger, and he went to my father again, and my father paid. And so when he asked me once again to come back, I knew what he was up to and I said "no". And he offered me ... Khatijah,' he said shamefacedly.

Osman was shocked. Already offering her to people? And no doubt if Kit Siang had agreed, Yusuf would have forced Khatijah in whatever way was necessary. He sighed.

'I didn't take it,' Kit Siang assured him. 'I mean, *Cik* Khatijah, she's a lot older than me, and it wouldn't be ... I mean it wasn't ...' After floundering a bit, he stopped speaking, assuming Osman would understand, and he did.

'And he got mad, he didn't want me to leave his place, you see. He wanted me to lose again,' he said, humiliated even in retrospect. 'And then he'd go to my father and take more and more money. Even if I were a good player, he'd make sure I'd never win.' (Osman surmised that Kit Siang being a good player was a big 'if'.)

'And then ...' Osman prompted.

'And then ... well, that night, I followed him when he went to Ruslan's house and then when he went home. I pulled him over on Jalan Tengku Cik, on the street, and told

him to leave me alone. He just took my hands off his shirt,

picked me right up off the ground and put me down a little ways away. 'Don't make me do more than that,' he said to me. 'You'll regret it.'

'Did people see you talking to him?'

'I guess.' Kit Siang shrugged miserably. 'They were probably laughing at me.'

Osman shook his head. 'I don't think so. Go on.'

'He didn't want to hit me, you see, because it would leave a mark and my father would be angry. He didn't want that. He laughed at me.' Osman could see how wounding that would be for a boy of Kit Siang's age. 'And then he walked away, down toward the river. He was never afraid of me. He never thought I would ever do anything to him. Or could, really. So I followed him again, and I saw ...' Here he began to pale, and his father encouraged him to tell the whole story.

'I saw someone come out and push him into the mud. It was dark, really dark, and I couldn't see who it was, but maybe a woman.'

He looked close to tears now, and Osman would have ordered him some tea, but didn't want to interrupt the flow. 'He fell hard, and the killer put his foot – her foot? – anyway, a foot on his face to keep him under water. Then she left, and I went over ...' He took a deep breath. 'And I put my foot on his face, too, to make sure he was really dead.'

His story complete, he burst into tears and sat crying into his father's shoulder. He sobbed for a few moments and then picked up his head, accepting the fistful of tissues Osman thrust at him.

'I was scared, and I didn't want to tell anyone, but I had to.' He sniffed. 'I guess I go to jail now,' he said morosely, and Ah Pak's hand tightened on his shoulder. Osman cleared his throat.

'I'm glad you came to tell me. It was the honest thing to do. And brave, too. A lot of people would have hoped that no one ever found out, but you came and told the truth, and your father should be very proud of you.'

Ah Pak nodded, but now looked even paler. It took a lot of courage, Osman realized, to put your family at risk this way, but it would cathartic for everyone when the story was finally no dark family secret.

'But you see,' Osman continued, 'you didn't kill him. He was dead already. You just showed how angry you were, but you're no killer.'

Osman couldn't be too sure about this, but he thought he was probably right. Enough people were suffering to free themselves of Yusuf. He wouldn't ruin this young man's life. Yusuf finally got what was coming to him, he thought, though it certainly wasn't the way a policeman should think. He brushed the thought away. He thought Azrina would approve.

'Thank you,' he said to Ah Pak. 'Thank you for coming in. I will call you if we need more information.' He stood up behind his desk.

Ah Pak seemed stunned. 'He doesn't have to stay here?'

'No. Why? He's committed no crime.'

'You don't think …'

'I do not,' Osman said firmly. 'Go home and plan your

wedding. You are getting married, aren't you? I heard it from *Mak Cik* Maryam.'

He nodded violently. 'Yes. Yes, I am.'

Osman smiled. 'Good luck,' he said. 'I got married myself last year.'

He gave Kit Siang a man-to-man smile and walked them out the door. Ah Pak clasped his hand, and looked as though he might hug him. 'Thank you,' he said. 'Thank you for giving me my boy back.'

It was a good day's work.

# Chapter XXXI

'While you were off,' Mamat grumbled, 'I just didn't have the heart to show Borek anymore, and Ah Pak was so ... distracted. But now, I think I can pay attention to my birds again, don't you?' Maryam agreed definitively.

'I'm thinking of Bacok. There's a big tournament, I mean the biggest one in Kelantan, there in two weeks. But I don't know.' The enthusiasm in his face dimmed. 'It's too far on a motorbike with the birds in cages. They could catch a chill or be upset by the wind or the noise.'

He looked worried. Maryam thought it all too typical that he was concerned about how the birds would take it, not how she would. This was not the time for her to complain, however; she was relieved to have things back to the way they were in a happier past. Mamat's plan had worked, and though nothing was ever said – neither 'I'm sorry' nor 'I forgive you' – it was now understood that this is what was *meant,* and all was well. Now, she would not upset her husband for any reason.

'I have an idea,' she said slowly, thinking it through. 'I think the police owe me a favour, don't you? I think I'll ask Rahman if he can drive us in the car. And maybe Aliza should come, just to help out. What do you think?'

Mamat gave her a long look. 'Do you think it's a good idea for Aliza to come?'

'Why not? We'll both be there. It isn't as though she'll be unchaperoned.'

'I really must pay attention to the birds,' he warned her. 'I can't play matchmaker when I'm at a contest, you know.'

As though that would be more important than a possible match for your daughter! The bird fancier in Mamat seemed to have gotten the better of the father in him, and a year ago, Maryam would have made that clear to him. But now?

'Well, of course, you need to take care of the birds, but I'll keep her close to me. And it will give them a chance to see if they really like each other. Wouldn't you prefer to have a car take us? The birds would be protected, and it might mean you can be in Bacok instead of maybe not being able to go.' She smiled beatifically at him, full of the pride of one who has put someone else's well-being before her own.

Azrina walked quickly through Kampong Penambang, willing for no one to see her or comment upon her presence there. For her husband's sake, and for her own edification, she would need to understand the *hala*, and how it might have affected Osman. Maryam was cured, and Azrina was glad for it, but she worried for Osman and feared he might again fall into illness. And she was determined to avoid that.

She did not stop to see Maryam or Rubiah, but went straight to Pak Lah's house and found him sitting quietly on his porch, smoking a cigarette and constructing a rattan bird cage. He smiled at her when he saw her and began to rise, though she begged him to remain comfortable.

'Pak Lah,' she began haltingly, already somewhat embarrassed at her request, 'My husband, *Che* Osman, was also ill at the same time *Mak Cik* Maryam became sick. Feverish, frightened, restless: I thought it might be *kempunan*, wanting something so badly you fall ill if you don't get it.

'*Kempunan* for what?' Pak Lah interrupted gently.

'To solve the case. To know what happened. To get to the truth. All these things, that's what he wanted. And, of course, in this case, things were so … murky for so long. I think that's what made him sick. Or maybe the *hala*,' she added doubtfully. 'I mean, such a strong spirit, maybe it affected him somehow …'

She stopped talking and looked imploringly at Pak Lah, who merely nodded and waited for her to continue. She cleared her throat. 'Do you think that could have made him sick? The *hala*, I mean – do you think it wanted *him* too?'

Pak Lah smiled at her. 'The *hala* is very strong, as you saw,' he began. 'If the *hala* wanted him, we would have seen much more than just a fever. Look at *Mak Cik* Maryam, and she's a very strong woman, inside and out. And even she was taken over by the *hala* spirit. So I say again, if it wanted *Che* Osman, you would know.

'Things might be different here than in Perak,' he told her, casting no aspersions on her home state while doing so. 'I believe here in Kelantan, we have *hala* spirits and were-tigers both.

'A *hala* spirit,' he said, leaning back against his house while his wife served coffee and snacks, 'it's a strong one. People who have a *hala* character need to express it, and it's difficult, you see. They long to act like a tiger: to be strong and fierce, to roar and sometimes pounce. How can you do that in a *kampong*?'

He smiled, both at the thought of a Malay villager pouncing on anyone in the course of an average day and with pleasure in talking about the realm of the supernatural, about which his knowledge was vast and accurate.

'Of course, you can't,' he continued, enjoying his role as lecturer. 'You'd upset everyone. So, what to do if you have that sort of spirit? *Silat*, Malay martial arts, maybe – if you can learn and you have time, or become a soldier, maybe a policeman.' He nodded at her, but she could not see where this applied to Osman: was that why he had become sick? Perhaps he just didn't have the right character for it. She put that thought out of her mind as disloyal, and frankly, irrelevant. He had many other qualities, such as intelligence and tenacity, which more than made up for the dearth of *hala* spirit.

As though he read her mind, Pak Lah continued her train of thought. 'Don't worry, *Cik* Na, it might even be better if your husband isn't a *hala*. It means he has more control of his anger. Or he may even have less anger to begin with, and that's a good thing.

'Then, some people are *hala* and actually turn into tigers, real tigers, at night. They say – that is, people say – that Korinci people from Sumatra are like that, and if you peek at them just before daybreak, you can see them turning back from tigers to people. It's dangerous, though, because if they catch you while they're still tigers, they can kill you. Tigers are dangerous, in their spirits and their bodies.'

'Are they all killers?'

'Many of them.' He looked thoughtful. 'I should say, most of them. Real tigers, not the spirit tigers, they kill to eat; it's just their nature, neither good nor bad. Most of them stay well away from people. Were-tigers now, they'll kill just to kill. They'll eat what they kill most of time, just like tigers, but don't fear people, not at all. And they'll kill them without a second thought.

'It's a perilous thing,' he mused, 'playing with tigers. You've seen it here yourself.' He waved his hand over the coffee, inviting her to drink.

'Now your husband and his illness. Well, let me see. It could be *kempunan*, it could be a spirit which could attack him because he was weakened by just such a longing. It's possible. Shall I see him?'

'No, wait,' Azrina said nervously. She had no idea how Osman would react to seeing Pak Lah come to cure him. 'Let me speak to him first.'


Noriah grew more listless, and yet more restless, by the day. She took to wandering around the *kampong* looking lost and ever older. At first, her neighbours would stop her and ask where she

233

wanted to go, and when she couldn't answer, they would guide her home and make her tea. But as it became a daily occurrence, more often they left her to her own devices as she followed her own compass and prowled the village alleys, staring emptily at nothing until hunger drove her back to the house.

A young relative had been nominated to take care of the house until Noriah regained her composure, and she would try to feed her when she returned from her meanderings, but Noriah was unresponsive, and people whispered that she had lost her mind. Or maybe laboured under an evil spell.

Sometimes she wouldn't come home at all for an entire day, and then for several days, though her son would look for her only in a haphazard way. People sensed he was happy enough not to find her, and begrudged spending any time on her at all. It appeared that Noriah was now set adrift from this world and inhabited only her own, and that world seemed a very colourless and unhappy place.

# Chapter XXXII

Maryam accepted Azrina's explanation of the second 'tiger' killing. It held together, she had to admit, and it seemed a likely course of action for the Thais. Having killed once with a nail-studded board, it would be fitting justice for one of them to be killed in the same horrible fashion. And she believed the Thais would never be found. No one in Thailand was actually looking for them, and as Azrina had described, they could easily disappear in their own country and never emerge. There would be no evidence for or against this theory. You either believed it or you didn't.

And yet ... part of her thought that second killing was the tiger she had seen. It wasn't just that she didn't want to think she was mad, though that fear gnawed at her. The tiger was so real, she could still conjure up the feel of him under her hand, his advice, his low growl. How could he be so real to her and not be real indeed? She didn't believe it possible.

And the riddle he'd given her, supposedly identifying the killer ... she still could not make sense of it. It certainly hadn't come from her, there were no recesses of her mind where she stored such thoughts. She brooded over it, trying to fit reality to the tiger's words. How did Khatijah 'push riches away, yet gather them'? Was Siti Hawa the treasure, and pushing riches away was working in a gambling den? Weak yet strong: that was easy. Despised, yes – but respected? Yes, perhaps she had earned their respect when they had really known her, but despised her earlier. Maybe that was the explanation.

Maryam was angry at herself for even remembering this message. She was a detective, not a philosopher, and unsuited to unraveling these cryptic utterances which had not only been of no help at all in finding the killer, they had actually misled her into suspecting Ah Pak. She could not mention these reflections to anyone else, for doing so would be an admission she had thought about the tiger, and she could not afford that again. She would never be forgiven for it.

And there had been her own descent into tigerhood, which had given her such exaltation and shown her another way of experiencing the world. She also recalled the horror with which she came back to herself, muddy and unkempt by the riverbank, filthy from walking on all fours. How could both of these have happened if the tiger never existed, if *hala* were only a story and had no place walking the earth? It must have been real, though she had decisively foresworn any more communication with *hala*, or *any* tigers real or human. The tiger had not helped her, he had hindered her, and nearly destroyed her. It was a world she wanted no part of.

But it continued to haunt her. Livestock had been found

mauled in Kampong Penambang, bearing all the hallmarks of a tiger in the vicinity looking for easy pickings among domestic animals. There was no talk of *hala* now; this appeared to be typical tiger behavior, with no supernatural overtones, and though it was quite rare for them to hunt in populated areas, in was not entirely without precedent. The men in the village together dug a tiger trap near the river: a deep pit with sharpened bamboo spikes at the bottom, well-covered with grass and leaves. At night, meat would be left in it to lure a tiger to its death, impaled on the poles.

Children were constantly warned to stay far from the pit, with gruesome descriptions of the fate of unwary boys who fell in by accident. The stories were hair-raising enough to keep the majority of the *kampong*'s youngsters far away from going anywhere near it, and even the coterie of daredevils who always sparked mischief decided to court trouble elsewhere.

Maryam thought Yi was too old to be exploring the river any more, but Aliza gave him a lecture which made it clear that if she found him anywhere near the trap, he'd be better off throwing himself in it than facing the punishment she'd have in store for him. He seemed to take this warning to heart.

And meanwhile, the attacks on Kampong Penambang's geese and goats continued. People occasionally claimed to have heard a roar in the night, or unfamiliar rustling, but no one had seen the tiger, who kept away from the pit, preferring to hunt rather than receive easy carrion. No one dared to walk at night and risk meeting the tiger, and everyone began taking special care to keep the animals safe, even building cages for the goats on their porches to keep them free from harm.

Maryam was particularly reluctant to have anything to do with tigers of any stripe, and kept closer to home than was her wont in the evenings. She longed to see her grandchildren, only a short walk away, but she and Mamat absolutely forbade Ashikin to leave her house at night. And as for taking innocent young children into a now dangerous darkness ... that was simply unthinkable. Maryam felt her world becoming smaller and more threatening and was, in fact, heartily sick of tigers and hoped never to think about them again.

And finally, the trap worked. Towards dawn, when the last stars were fading, the *kampong* was awakened by a roar: one that comprised rage, surprise and sorrow. It continued, turning into what seemed like a wail, and the men rushed to the pit and clawed away the leaves that kept them from seeing clearly into their trap, though the keening sounds continued, and they saw their tiger.

Several of the men could not credit what they saw, nor could they reconcile the roar they heard with what lay before them. Noriah, impaled on the stakes, letting go of a life she no longer wanted. Some people claimed she still had a tiger's tail when they found her and was not yet completely human, others said they saw nothing of the sort. Maryam exchanged a long look with Pak Lah, which needed no words to make it clearer: here was the result of his spell, falling back on Noriah, who had sent it to Maryam.

The kampong buzzed with news of Noriah's death: indeed, it

seemed all of Kelantan discussed nothing else. Prominent citizen revealed as were-tiger! Evil spell returned to sender! People did not even pretend to mourn, rather they dug straight into the details of her death and the evil magic she practiced.

Maryam and Rubiah refused to participate any of these discussions. Maryam devoutly wished it would be forgotten, and were-tigers with it. She felt lucky to have escaped the curse which imprisoned her, and had no wish to revisit that particular hell, even in conversation. At first, her neighbours asked eagerly about it, but they soon learned she would not talk, and they gave up, preferring to speculate among themselves. If you were ever in its throes, Maryam thought, a touch bitterly, you'd never want to hear about it again.

She threw her considerable energies into her family, who were delighted, by and large to receive her undivided attention. With the tiger scare over, they had taken back the night, walking as they always had before to Ashikin's house to see the children, visiting neighbours, seeing Rubiah and her family. Maryam was grateful to regain her mind, and thankful, more than thankful, to have taken back her life, her family, her world.

# Kain Songket Mysteries

## Shadow Play (Vol.1)

*Shadow Play* is the first in the series of Kain Songket Mysteries set in the northern state of Kelantan, Malaysia, during the 1970s. Mak Cik Maryam, a *kain songket* (silk) trader in Kota Bharu Central Market, discovers a murder in her own backyard, shattering the bucolic village world she thought surrounded her. While the new Chief of Police, a pleasant young man from Ipoh whose mother's admonitions about the wiles of Kelantanese girls still ring in his ears, wrestles with the bewildering local dialect, Maryam steps up to solve the mystery herself. Her investigation brings her into the closed world of the *wayang kulit* shadow play theater and the lives of its performers—a world riven by rivalries and black magic. Trapped in a tangle of jealousy, Maryam struggles to make sense of the crime in spite of the spells sent to keep her from secrets long buried and lies woven to shield the guilty.

• Winner - Best Debut Novel
SBPA Book Awards (Singapore, 2012)

• Shortlisted - English Fiction
Popular–The Star Readers' Choice Awards (Malaysia, 2013)

## Princess Play (Vol.2)

Mak Cik Maryam is plunged once again into the shadowy world of murder, hatred and madness when a fellow market woman is killed after a successful *main puteri* (princess play) curing ceremony. Suddenly, the villagers she thought she knew reveal secrets she never suspected, while her good sense and solid courage lead her to unmask the murderer among them. Follow Mak Cik Maryam in the second Kelantanese murder case in the Kain Songket Mysteries series.

• Shortlisted - English Fiction
Popular–The Star Readers' Choice Awards (Malaysia, 2014)